FEAR OF DARK WATER

OTHER NOVELS BY PATRICIA BOW

Wib Willett and the Tombstone Club

Sally Sharp and the Corduroy Clue

Storm Watch

The Hangman's Garden

Lynx Leap

Running on Moonlight

The Starry Window *

* Book 3 of Passage to Mythrin

A GOBLIN POSTMAN CHILLER

FEAR OF

DARK WATER

PATRICIA BOW

Published by Patricia Bow
www.execulink.com/~thebows/patricia.htm

Distributed by Lulu Press
www.lulu.com

This book was first published in 2006 by Cora Verlag GmbH under the title *Im Bann der Wasserhexe*, in German translation. *Fear of Dark Water* is the author's original (but revised and expanded) English text.

Goblin Postman icon created by Patricia Bow

Cover image: "Little Waterfall" by Jim Naureckas of edenpictures, adapted and used in accordance with his Creative Commons license. https://www.flickr.com/photos/edenpictures/8331071253/

Chapter 1

JO WAVED a drift of exhaust fumes away from her face and looked around for the welcoming committee. There was not a sign of one, not a single person there to meet her, and it wasn't as if they'd be lost in the crowd. MacPhee, population 452, had no crowd.

The main street was deserted except for herself and two small boys. Herself, standing on the sidewalk in front of Bob's Seed, Feed and Hardware with her luggage around her like sheep around their shepherd. The boys, sitting on a wooden bench outside the MacPhee General Store across the street. They were staring at Jo as if they'd never seen an unfamiliar face before, and licking ice cream cones. A scruffy mongrel dog sat at their feet, gazing hopefully from cone to cone.

The only other moving things Jo could see were the intercity bus lumbering westward up the road toward Flesherton and Owen Sound, and its dust cloud, a tall golden plume in the slanted light of a summer evening.

"It's so quiet," she whispered. Even the leaves on the chestnut trees in front of the store hung motionless. Living in a constantly growing, changing city like Waterloo, you could forget there were places so still. In her apartment overlooking King Street, over the last few years she'd gotten used to the beep and hum of traffic, the bang and roar of roadwork, the chatter when the clubs let out. She hoped she would be able to sleep tonight without that lullaby in her ears.

Here, it was as if the whole world was holding its breath. Even on the south shore of Nova Scotia, where the immensity of sky and sea reduced everything human to a footnote — even there it was never like this. There the winds were always sweeping in and out, and the ocean was a living presence, breathing, never asleep.

In a moment she was there, in that memory box behind her eyelids. There on the shore below the cliffs, with their caves and their hidden dark pools. Their sucking waters.

No. She shook her head hard. *No dark waters here.* She took three evenly spaced deep breaths, slowly in through the nose and blown out through the mouth.

Then focussed on what was in front of her eyes. The old buildings, old enough to be charming if they weren't so shabby. The original red and white paint on the general store's sign weathered to pinkish beige under recent black touch-ups. (General store! Could this be genuine? Would it have a cracker barrel?) A single pickup truck rumbling past, kicking up more dust. The boys with their ice cream cones, still licking, still staring.

That was reality, here and now. Not the other.

Those cones did look tempting. Jo's throat was dry, her short hair spiky with sweat. She could feel it sticking up all over her head when she scrubbed her hands through it. *I must look like a red-quilled porcupine!*

She was thinking of lugging her bags over to the general store and going in, exploring a bit and buying a cone, and some water too, when another dust cloud appeared in the distance down the road eastward. A minute later a big red Ford station wagon rattled into view. A thin arm waved out the passenger side window. The car made a U-turn and stopped with a screech of aging brakes alongside her.

The passenger door flew open and a little girl jumped out in a flurry of tanned bare arms and legs. "Are you Josephine Meurig?"

"Yes, that's — "

"You're here! You actually came!" The child ran at Jo as if to hug her, then stopped short and took a step back. Her eyes ran over Jo from top to bottom, probing, appraising, hopeful.

Jo returned the appraising look. The "child" was not a little girl after all. Despite her size and childlike delicacy she was closer to sixteen, possibly seventeen. "You're from Spinbrook House?"

"Yeah! I'm Mel," said the girl. She was all hair and eyes, and could have used a few more pounds on her, Jo thought. Mel had tied her clouds of dark hair up into a high pony tail. Fine tendrils clung to her damp cheeks. Tiny, pretty, dainty as painted porcelain, with dark smudges under the big coffee-brown eyes that made them look even bigger. She made Jo, usually comfortable at a slim five-foot-nine, feel as clumsy as a Clydesdale.

"Aunt Frieda's busy, so I came instead." Mel looked over her shoulder. "And that's Calvin. Calvin Ransom. He helps out around the place."

Calvin had climbed quietly out of the car and begun hoisting Jo's bags into the trunk. He didn't stop moving, just gave her a look — a flash of sky-blue eyes — and a nod. A shock of corn-silk hair spilled over his face as he bent to scoop up the last of her luggage, two well-stuffed gym bags in one hand. The weight gave him no trouble, she noticed. He looked young, not much more than her own twenty-three. Tall too, which was nice.

"We might as well get back," Mel said, without enthusiasm.

"Is it far?"

"Couple miles. Why?"

"I've been stuffed in a bus for three hours!" Jo stretched her arms and flexed her stiff shoulders. "The last two hours I was squished between the window and a three-hundred-pound hamburger fiend.

Who brought his own food. And hadn't showered. I could really use a walk and a breath of fresh air. Do you mind?"

"'Course not." Mel turned to Calvin, but he was already back in the driver's seat, having said not a word but apparently caught everything. He gave Jo another sky-blue look and put the car in drive.

"Wow," said Jo appreciatively, when he was out of sight. "So he helps out? Is he always that quiet?"

"Calvin? Yeah, he's not real chatty." Mel started down the street westward, in the opposite direction from where the station wagon had gone. "Shortcut's this way," she explained. "There's some woods, then a stream with a bridge, and then the house."

After five minutes of brisk walking the last house was behind them. The road stretched ahead westward, a golden pathway of reflected light. Walls of tall trees pressed close on both sides. Jo tried to identify the trees. Pines, cedars, maples, birches, and more she didn't know. It was still uncannily quiet. There wasn't a car on the road as far as the eye could see, not a farm house in sight, not another human being besides themselves.

Mel walked with her hands bunched in the pockets of her shorts, eyes studying the asphalt. Jo wondered why she'd seemed so glad to see her — her, a total stranger. *You actually came!* And then the aborted hug. The girl seemed almost desperate at that moment. Now she seemed glum.

"What a beautiful place!" Jo filled her lungs with fresh, resin-scented air. It was so clean it almost prickled. Like downing a glass of cold ginger ale. "Must be really healthy, living here," she ventured, and instantly knew how inane that sounded. She thought back to her own mid-teen years, though that seemed centuries ago now. "What, um, what do you do with your time? Are there other kids your age? I mean, people to hang with?"

"No," Mel said crossly. "Anyway I don't live here, I'm just staying here for the summer, while my parents are away. They're off in Australia team-teaching bioethics at the University of Sydney. They said I'd be bored in Sydney, would you believe, and so here I am having the time of my life with the wolves and the bears, and not even a phone!" She detoured to gather a small stone with her sandalled foot and kicked it savagely along the road. "Can you believe I had to leave my phone and my laptop behind? Doesn't that totally suck? I'm too wired, my mom says! I need a break from electronics, I'm rotting my brain, she says! Like she doesn't use a computer in her work!" She took a little run, caught up to the stone and kicked it again.

Jo picked the important bit out of the torrent of exclamations. "Wolves and bears?" She darted a look into the sun-striped shadows under the trees. "Have you seen any?"

"No, but I've heard they're around." She gave Jo a questioning sideways look. "That's supposed to be part of the appeal, right? Being at Spinbrook House, I mean. The perfect house in the woods, civilization in the wilderness, all that stuff. And the water sounds, that's supposed to be really calming, right?"

"That's the idea." Jo squinted along the road. Heat waves shimmered up from the asphalt. "Where *is* the house?"

"Not far." After another few minutes of walking, not so brisk now, Mel said, "Are you, um, a soldier?"

"A soldier!" Astonished, Jo stopped and stared.

Mel stopped and stared back. "I thought you must be. I heard Aunt Frieda on her phone, something about PTSD. That's something soldiers get, right? And you're tall, like... So I thought..."

"I'm not a soldier." That was curt, so she added, "I work at the University of Waterloo. And no, I'm not a prof," she said, seeing Mel open her mouth to ask the obvious question. "I'm an admin person in environmental studies. I help undergrads register and adjust their schedules and so on."

"My God, that sounds boring."

"It usually isn't."

"Well, if you're not a soldier, how would you get PTSD?"

"Tell you what." Jo flashed a brilliant smile. "We could do a trade of personal, private information. You know, like exchanging hostages. I'll tell you why I'm here, or some of it, and you tell me what's bothering you."

"Nothing's bothering me." Mel knotted her eyebrows, turned away and walked on.

"Okay, my mistake." She hoped Mel had taken the hint: *Back off.*

"I mean, aside from, you know, it's so dire and drab. Being here." Mel waved her hands as she walked. "I mean, I have friends in Etobicoke, that's where I live, why couldn't I stay with one of them? But oh no, blood is thicker than water, my dad says."

"Meaning?"

"He says I should stay with a relative. That's okay up to a point." Mel shook her head, making her clouds of hair drift on the air. "I mean, there's Aunt Frieda — she's nice, but she's always working, she's a graphic designer, and there's Uncle Harold, he's great when he's around — he's away right now — some business in the States. And there's Calvin, you've seen what a barrel of fun *he* is. Oh, and there's Lew."

"Who's Lew?"

"My cousin Lewis. He's only eight, and not much company. I mean, he's a sweetie, but it's depressing, being around him."

"Depressing? Why?"

"You'll see." Mel tilted her head toward the woods on their right.

"We go this way."

A dirt path branched away from the highway and into the woods. In ten steps they were in a different world. Shafts of bright gold sunlight striped on black blinked on and off across Jo's eyes. It was hard to see where they were going. Mel led the way, her conversation exhausted, and Jo shuffled along behind, squinting, glad of the white-painted stones that marked the edges of the path.

After a few minutes the path slanted downward. The slope cut off the gold of the sunlight, but the walking didn't become any easier. As Jo picked her way down, trying not to slip on the carpet of half-composted leaves, the woods darkened. A heavy silence muffled her steps. Each leaf hung motionless in the windless air. When noise did come, it was a faint silvery chiming. It took a minute for her to identify the sound of flowing water.

At the bottom of the hill the sound suddenly swelled. It burst around them as they stepped out from under the trees and found themselves standing two metres from white water. Upstream, to their left, a slim waterfall arced down, broke in white foam on a rock-studded slope and spread out into a wide, quiet pool. The pool narrowed again, overflowed, and bubbled downstream, a white snake twisting among rocks.

The sun was almost gone now, barely gilding the tops of trees high above. The sky overhead was peach-coloured, its glow more than bright enough to light their way.

"So this is the stream?" Jo looked down at the ribbon of water gurgling at her feet, then across at the forest-thick hillside. Then craned her neck to see upstream and down. "Where's the bridge?"

"This is the bridge." Mel grinned, her first real smile since Jo's arrival.

The "bridge" was a series of flat-topped stones that crossed the water at the point where it flowed out of the quiet pool and down into the narrow stretch of rapids. Across the stream, about five metres away, the path started again. It curved into the woods and uphill to the left, toward a crag overhanging the waterfall.

Jo took the stepping stones in her stride. She wasn't afraid of falling into the water — the stones were solid, and big and flat enough to stand on easily, and the space between them was no stretch for her long legs. But it was a new experience to walk across a whitewater stream. It was unsettling. The rush and spin of the water on her right made her feel as if she was sliding sideways. She felt slightly dizzy. Not daring to take the next step until her head cleared, she turned her back on the torrent, knelt down and looked into the still waters of the pool on the other side of the stepping stones.

"Jo?" Mel called from the far bank. "You coming?"

"Sure. Just a sec."

Strange sort of pool, Jo thought. Its surface should have mirrored the sky, but instead of shining peach it was inky black. She wondered how deep it was. No way to tell. You couldn't see down into the water, or not very far. She dipped a hand in and snatched it out again. The water was December-cold.

A small, icy lump formed in her stomach. She tried to laugh it away. Such a peaceful place, so unthreatening! And you could wade across this pond without getting your shoulders wet, she was willing to bet. Couldn't be more than three or four feet deep, surely. Out on the glassy surface, a water strider stepped in circular dints like tiny snowshoes. Nearer, a circle of cream-coloured foam turned lazily. Nothing there to be bothered about, nothing at all. You couldn't see anything in there, not even a bit of weed.

That was the trouble, of course. You couldn't see. Anything could be down there. Anything.

Or nothing! Snap out of it, Jo, use your head!

She tried to push herself up from her crouch, but no part of her wanted to unbend. Too long sitting on the bus, she thought. But it felt like more than that. Like weights pulling her down. Her wet hand ached with cold. Mel called again, sounding very far away now. It was so hard to move. And she felt so cold all over! Weird, on a warm evening like this.

Still in a half crouch, she froze. There was something in there after all. Something pale deep down in the dark water. It rose toward her, became an oval, a shape like…

"Hey!" Two hands grabbed her arm and shook it. She straightened up and blinked at Mel, then looked back down at the pool. No pale oval looked up at her. The dark surface lay unbroken. Sweat trickled down between her shoulder blades. She shivered.

"I, I thought I saw something in there." She stepped across the stones, careful not to look at the pool until they were safe on the far shore.

"A fish, probably. The stream is jumping with them. Well, let's not stand here all night. There it is, feast your eyes!" She swept an arm upward dramatically. "Spinbrook House!"

Jo gave her head a shake, blinked again, and looked up. For a moment all she could see was the craggy mass of rock and trees above the waterfall, a jagged black outline against the sky. Then a square of light appeared in the mass. Then another, and another. More and more squares lit up, until the crag took shape as a house with rows and rows of big golden windows.

Jo caught her breath. The house shone like a lantern over the waterfall. "Oh, Mel. I've never seen anything so gorgeous! And you've been living there!"

"Uh-huh."

"Oh, wow. Is it just as beautiful inside?"

Mel shaped a tight smile. "You'll have to make up your own mind about that."

Chapter 2

"AND THAT," said Frieda Stone, "is our hearthstone boulder. All you can see is the top of it, of course. Nine-tenths of it is down below where you can't see it, like an iceberg."

Jo knelt and ran a hand along the smooth, cold stone shelf that jutted up from the flagstone floor. *Like an iceberg* was right. She wished someone would light a fire in the man-high fireplace that opened in the living room wall above the shelf. Both wall and fireplace were built of layered shale, and looked like the side of a cliff.

"Most builders would have blasted the boulder out of the way." Mrs. Stone nudged the hearthstone fondly with the toe of one red-strapped sandal. "But this house was designed to be part of the landscape, so the boulder stayed. It's granite, you know, which makes it rather special in this spot. It's igneous rock that pushed up from the magma aeons ago, and all the surrounding rock is limestone, which is softer. Over the millennia the limestone eroded and left the granite pillar standing." She laughed, with a flash of very white teeth. "Can you tell I've researched it?"

Jo smiled back at her and turned on one heel to scan the huge living room. "So much glass! Windows everywhere."

"Yes, which makes it expensive to heat in the winter! Still, I love the windows. They make me feel the woods are right in here with us."

Spinbrook House was spare and luxurious at the same time. The floors of water-smoothed stone were spread with soft moss-coloured rugs. The centre of the house was open from top to bottom, with galleries running around the central well on the second and third floors, connected by an open spiral staircase. Columns of red Douglas fir soared to the roof, looking as if they had grown there and just had their branches and bark stripped off. Lights glowed from frosted glass niches in the ceilings and walls, like the sun behind clouds.

"It's awesome," Jo murmured, and meant it. She only wished it was a little warmer.

"It's awful," Mel muttered, from the depths of a brown leather chair. Jo didn't think Mrs. Stone heard.

Lewis did, though. He looked at Mel and his mouth curled mischievously. The smile almost made you forget his wheelchair, and the brace that held his body upright. They ought to take him out in the sun more, Jo decided. He was too pale, and that smile was too rare. Without it, he looked even younger than eight. His brown eyes were enormous in his thin face.

"Come on, Lew, you be the tour leader." Mrs. Stone began pushing Lew's wheelchair toward the all-glass side of the living room. "Melinda, are you coming?"

"No thanks."

"Oh, all right," Mel's aunt said cheerfully. "I guess it's all old hat to you now. Jo, I've saved the best for last. The Cataract Room."

Jo followed them to a shallow ramp cut into the living room floor. A steel gate closed it off at the top. At the bottom it ended at an archway in the glass wall. "The Cataract Room. It's called that because it hangs over the falls, right? Isn't that dangerous?"

"Oh, no. The room doesn't hang above the falls, not exactly, it's set on steel beams driven into the rock. It's absolutely secure, just like the rest of the house." As she spoke, Mrs. Stone unlatched the gate and swung it open, then eased the wheelchair down the ramp. When they reached the doorway in the glass wall, Lew made an urgent sound.

His mother bent over him. "Want to stop here?" He nodded quickly.

She locked the chair's wheels, then stepped past him and walked out into the room beyond. Jo followed cautiously. The roar of the waterfall surrounded her. The lights from the living room reflected off thick glass walls and curving glass roof. It was like being inside a bubble that floated in a midnight sea.

Jo took a few more steps and stopped. "The floor," she gulped.

The floor was glass too. Thick, greenish glass. Floodlights in the corners, aimed downward, lit up a blur of moving water only two or three inches beneath. Jo felt as if she was standing right on the surface of the torrent. She couldn't make herself move from that spot.

The stream poured almost the full length of the room from west to east. About half a metre short of the east wall, it curled over a lip of stone and dropped. Spray spattered the glass.

"Jo? Are you all right?"

"Um... yes, sure." Jo peeled her gaze from the floor under her feet and forced herself, heart thumping, to walk to the east end of the room, where Mrs. Stone was looking out. The haze of mist from the falls was lit to gold by the house lights.

"It's even better by moonlight," Mrs. Stone said. "It's very pretty then. And in the morning, the sun makes rainbows in the spray. Well? Do you like it?"

"I'm sure I will in the morning." Jo turned around. The living room doorway looked very far away, the glass floor twice as wide as before. Wicker chairs with pink floral-print cushions stood around looking comfortable, pretty and completely out of place, in her opinion. "But I can't imagine anybody coming here to relax."

"Harold does. He can sit here for hours after work and watch the water go by. I admit I like showing it to people — they're always impressed."

Jo tried not to look at the floor as they walked back toward the living room. It felt unsafe to put her feet down, as if the glass might crack at the next step.

She caught Lew's eye. He smiled encouragement from the doorway.

Closer to the house and farther away from the lip of the falls, the water moved more slowly. Jo breathed easier. In one place, right in front of Lew's wheelchair, the floor light showed a turning circle of foam, signaling a slow eddy next to the foundation wall. The eddy made her think of the dark pool. And, like the pool, here you couldn't see more than a couple of inches deep. She wondered if water rats ever came and looked up from that spot, or otters, or…

She was breathing faster, heart thumping, sweat prickling out above her eyes. A mistake, coming here.

Something pale lifted from the slow circle of foam and splayed itself against the underside of the glass floor. A dead leaf, tossed there by the current, Jo thought, as she took another step toward the spot. But that was the quiet place with the eddy. There was no turbulence there.

She was close enough then to see the thing clearly. Next moment it peeled from the glass and sank beneath the surface.

Chapter 3

JO STOOD AND shook. She couldn't move, couldn't take her eyes off that spot. Suppose that... thing... rose to the glass again, right under her feet?

"M... Mrs... Mrs. Stone…"

Mrs. Stone had already stepped back through the doorway and was pulling Lew's wheelchair around. As he turned he caught Jo's eye again. His face was paper-white.

He'd seen it too. The greenish-white wrist, the long, pointed fingers...

Jo gulped air, leaped over the spot, landed in the doorway, and ran up the ramp. "Mrs. Stone!"

Lew's mother let go of the wheelchair at the top of the ramp. "Jo, what's the matter?"

"Didn't you see that?"

"See what?"

"I saw — I thought I saw — " Jo pointed wildly. "Down there, under the floor — a — a hand — out of the water — "

"A hand?" Mrs. Stone looked bewildered. Across the room, Mel sat up in her chair and stared.

"On the underside of the glass. At first I thought it was a leaf — "

"Oh, then that's what it was." Mrs. Stone's face lit up with laughter. "Jo, nobody swims in that stream — it's far too cold! Besides, right above the falls would be dangerous."

"But," Jo began. Then she met Lew's scared eyes again, and bit off what she'd been about to say. *It didn't look like a live hand. It looked dead.* She couldn't say that with Lew listening. "I — I guess you're right," she ended lamely. "Silly of me."

"Never mind, it's easy to mistake what you see through that thick glass, especially at night." Mrs. Stone closed the gate at the top of the ramp. Then she looked around, a finger tapping her lips. "Now, what haven't you seen? Oh, of course!" She waved the finger cheerily. "The cellar. The base of our wonderful hearthstone."

"Um — " Mel bounced out of her chair and caught Jo by the wrist before she could answer. "Let's do that tomorrow, Aunt Frieda, okay?"

"But it's the only thing Jo hasn't seen."

"Yes, but I can tell she's really tired."

"Oh, I'm so sorry. Melinda, you're absolutely right. I should have realized." Mrs. Stone slapped her forehead and smiled at Jo. "I expect you just want to get to bed. Mel will take you up to your room. And do help yourself to a bedtime snack from the kitchen if you're hungry!"

"Actually, I don't feel ti— " Jo winced as the toe of Mel's sandal connected with her ankle. "I mean, I do feel a bit tired. But thanks for the tour, Mrs. Stone. I love the house." *Except the Cataract Room!*

"Great! But drop the 'Mrs,' okay? Call me Frieda. I'm not that much older than you!"

"Oh — you bet."

Jo let Mel drag her up the spiral stairs to the third-floor gallery. "What was that about?" she hissed.

Mel put a finger to her lips and pushed open the second of three doors in the wall on her left, pulled her inside, and closed the door. Then she spun off and swung out an arm. "So this is your room!"

Jo could have guessed that, seeing her bags lined up in a row along one wall. "Okay, now what — "

"You don't want to see the cellar by night," Mel said firmly.

"Why not? Will I see dead hands come clawing through the floor?"

"What the heck are you ranting about?"

"The hand I saw — " Jo took a deep breath, in and out. "I'm sure I saw it," she muttered, now not quite so sure. The memory had an unreal, nightmarish quality. Maybe her eyes had been playing tricks on her. *Only, Lew saw it too. I'm sure he did.*

"Trust me." Mel flopped on the bed, face up. "This place will have you jumping out of your skin in no time. Probably not the best place for a person with PTSD."

Jo took another deep breath. *I'm calm.* She smiled to reinforce the calmness. *I'm cool. Mel is just yanking my chain. I'm going to have a nice time here. It's a beautiful house in a beautiful place. And this is a beautiful room.*

She looked around. It was a beautiful room. Floor of water-worn flagstones, a big bed spread with a colourful quilt, and a dark blue ceiling studded with a dozen tiny lights, like stars. One wall, the one opposite the door, was all glass, with a sliding door in the middle with a screen behind it. There was a pane you could open in the top half of the door. It was down now, letting in the cool evening air and the sounds of wind and water.

Mel jumped off the bed and slid open the glass door and screen. A stone-floored terrace ran the length of the building past all the windows. "That's Lew's room on the right." Mel pointed one way, then the other. "I'm on the left."

"Handy for midnight picnics, this terrace." Jo leaned on the chest-high iron railing beside Mel and breathed in the scent of fresh leaves and wet stone, and some kind of night-blooming flower she didn't recognize. She had to admit it smelled better than dumpsters and gasoline fumes.

This high above the falls, the water's roar was muted. Twenty feet below, the house lights glittered on flying spray and gilded the wet leaves on the edges of trees across the stream. Behind the outer bright layer of foliage, the woods melted away into blackness.

"It's terrible about Lew," she said. "I see why you say it's depressing, being around him. It's so sad, to see a kid his age in a wheelchair."

"Yeah. Especially since he wasn't always like that. He was fine until about a year ago. Then he started getting sicker and sicker."

"But what's wrong with him?"

"They don't know, that's the problem. The doctors have done all kinds of tests. Nothing. Big mystery. This summer, especially, he's really gone downhill. When I came here in July, he could feed himself. Now he can't even sit up by himself. He's too weak even to talk."

"So how does he tell people what he wants?"

"He doesn't. He's not strong enough to write, either. He's in his own little world."

"That's not right." Jo frowned. "Maybe if you worked with him, you know, physiotherapy — I could help — "

"Jo." Mel's voice was flat. "It's no good. Lew won't live to grow up. I heard the doctor say that to Aunt Frieda."

"But she... seems so..."

"Yeah. She's real good at faking, right? You'd think nothing's wrong at all, if you listen to her." After a moment she added, "He may not even live past Christmas."

Jo couldn't trust herself to speak. She wrapped her hands around the iron railing and gazed into the woods. It was a minute before she stopped seeing Lew's thin, smiling face and began seeing what was there.

"So that's why you're feeling down," she said at last. "It's Lew, isn't it?"

Mel crossed her wrists on the iron railing and rested her cheek on her forearms. "It's more than that."

"What, then?"

"I don't know."

"Really?" Jo gave her shoulder a nudge. "Is that the best you can do? Look, why don't we make a game of it?"

Mel raised her head and gave her an incredulous look. "A game!"

"Right," Jo said cheerfully. "To see who'll be the first to guess the other's secret fear."

"That's twisted!" Mel almost laughed. "So how will we play this game? What will the loser have to pay?"

"Um… She'll have to do what she's afraid of. How's that?"

"Fine by me. There's no way you'll guess my secret fear." Mel laughed now, but it was not a happy sound. "Because I don't know it myself. All I know is, there's something wrong. I'm scared. And I can't go home. I can't even text my best friend about it because I have no fracking phone!"

"You could write your friend a letter. Writing things out helps."

"Write a letter!" Mel hooted. "Oh sure, let's go back to the nineteenth century!"

"Twentieth."

"Whatever, it's a lifetime ago for me." Which, Jo realized, was true.

"Hey," Mel said meditatively. "You have a phone, right? Could I borrow..."

Jo was shaking her head. "Sorry. Left mine at home. All part of the plan for seeking peace in nature."

"Then I'm doomed!" Mel dropped her head back on her fore-arms.

"Come on, it can't be that bad."

"Yes it can!"

Let her stew, Jo told herself. A cool breeze had started up and the house lights caught the flick of moving leaves across the stream. She wondered if there were animals in there: rabbits, foxes, maybe bears. Or even wolves. "Are there," she began, and then bit it off. A pale oval looked out at her from the edge of the wood. "What's that?"

Mel peered. "Calvin, probably. He's out in the woods a lot. Cal-vin!" she called.

The pale oval floated in the darkness as if it had no body. It made Jo think of the dark pool, and whatever she'd seen there, or imagined she'd seen. The floating face. And the hand on the underside of the glass floor. Her fingers tightened on the railing. Her heart thumped.

"Calvin?" Mel called. "Calvin!"

The pale oval faded back into the dark. Nothing showed there now. Nobody answered. The rising night wind stirred the trees into a long sigh.

"Why would Calvin be lurking around the woods at night?" Jo demanded.

"I dunno."

"Does he live at Spinbrook House?"

"Yeah, for the summer. His family lives in MacPhee. He doesn't stay in the house, though. He has a room over the garage."

"Then it must be him." *Of course it was him! Who else could it be?*

Chapter 4

CALVIN PAUSED for a breather in the woods across from the house. The two girls were out on the third-floor terrace. He could see their heads against the bright window. Especially the new girl — sorry, woman — Jo. Real carrot-top, that one. Her backlit hair made a red-gold halo around her head.

Redheads were supposed to be all passion and temper, but she didn't look it. She looked more down-to-earth, steady. Not like Melanie, all nervous and antsy. A smile in the eyes. Bit of a stubborn look around the mouth. Not a bad way to be if you were staying in Spinbrook House.

He backed away from the edge of the stream. Someone called through the noise of the falling water, but he was in no mood for shouted conversation. On he went, feeling his way uphill through the tree-crowded darkness to the highway, then back to the village, walking fast.

He could have stopped by at home. His mother would have fed him enough and then some, his father would have sat him down to watch the news and rehash it, his kid sister would have hung on his arm and teased him for a game of ping pong. All good and normal things. Or he could have stopped by the twenty-four-hour gas station, where Kyle was working the night shift, and they would've talked of sane, normal things like baseball and job prospects and girls.

He didn't stop. Sanity and normality would jar tonight. He had nothing to say, nothing they would have understood, and they would have noticed. His mother especially, with her eagle eye for trouble.

And she would have worried herself sleepless.

Just have to settle for bone-tired instead of sane.

He walked straight through MacPhee, past the church and the antique shop — it didn't take long — and out the other side, away from the Spin River and Spinbrook House. On the nearly empty road, in the moonlight, his sneakers beat time and his thoughts spun out clear and cold.

That Jo. Should he warn her? Tell her to go while the going was good? But what could he say? He didn't have words for what he feared. And if he did she wouldn't believe him.

He walked until his legs went numb, then turned left down a side road, then left again, and headed back. The moon coursed ahead of him like a big white dog.

Funny! Once upon a time, he would have steered clear of Spinbrook House. You couldn't have paid him enough to work there. Yet now it seemed the right thing to do. Face your fears — wasn't that the right thing? Face them and beat them down.

Only, his fears weren't exactly melting away before him. Maybe tonight wouldn't be so bad, though. He hoped. As he turned at last from the county road onto the gravel drive that led to the house, he felt almost too tired to trudge the last few hundred yards.

Maybe tonight he'd be tired enough to sleep. Maybe, please God, this time he'd fall so deep asleep that the nightmares wouldn't be able to reach him.

JO SAT CROSS-LEGGED on her bed and admired her brand-new journal. Dr. Klein had offered one from a stack she kept on her desk, a plain hard-covered black notebook with half an inch of ruled pages inside, but Jo had bought this one herself. She loved the soft feel of the faux leather cover, the gleam of gilt on the page edges, the new smell of the thick, smooth paper.

Opening the book to the first page, she wrote her name in crisp black ink with a fine-tipped gel pen. Then flipped the page over and wrote today's date, July 31, at the top.

I bought myself this book, she wrote, *with the idea that having a nice blank book would make it easier to write about hard things. I doubt that now. I'm scared to begin. I made a promise to Dr. Klein, and to myself, that I would only write the truth, and as much of the truth as I can bear, and that I will keep trying, no matter how hard it is. Also, I won't cross anything out or tear out any pages. No matter how stupid it sounds, or how awful.*

I'll start by writing about things that aren't so hard. To begin with, Spinbrook House is not what I expected. Of course I knew how it would look from the pictures on its website, and I was prepared for the sense of isolation, I think. The quiet and the smell of the air — so organic and at the same time so pure — they took me by surprise at first, though they shouldn't have. I've been out in the woods and wild country before. All the same I was slightly stunned by it all for a bit. But I think it's growing on me.

I'm the only guest, right now. Frieda Stone, who seems very nice, takes paying guests one or two at a time. It's a family-style setup, which is fine with me. I'll make my own breakfast and if I wish I can help with other meals. So I was expecting a very peaceful, normal, ordinary sort of place, I mean ordinary aside from the setting.

What I wasn't prepared for – I think it comes from the people. Especially Mel, Frieda's niece, and Lew, her son. Lew is only eight and he's so ill. Mel says he's dying. I can't bear to think of it. Mel is troubled by something, and it may be the usual angst of age sixteen, but it seems like more.

All in all, I'm not so sure staying here is going to help me much.

But I'm not giving up so soon. Even though I haven't made a good start. There's this dark pool in the stream near the house, and it looks deep, but of course that's silly – a little stream like that. And there was another thing I thought I saw in the house, but it can't have been what it looked like.

Okay, no self-censorship. This is what I saw. Just a hour or so ago they were showing me the Cataract Room, this amazing room all glass, built out over the waterfall, and...

Her slanting script dashed across the page, filling line after line. She finished the first page and the one facing, and flipped to the third. *Speaking of secret fears,* she wrote, *I wish I hadn't made that stupid bargain with Mel. I told her we'd make a game of it, guess each other's secret fear. I was trying to help her, but maybe I was undermining myself – something I seem to be really good at these days. Telling my deepest pain to this journal is one thing, telling Mel is another. I barely know her. I don't know how receptive or understanding she is. If she's anything like Graeme, I couldn't possibly tell her what I'm afr—*

Jo lifted her pen from the page and stared. Written words were appearing on the blank right-hand page, opposite what she'd just written. Gliding on, letter after letter, all by themselves. *what... I'm... afraid... of.*

The writing was spiky and upright, not at all like her own. The ink was dark blue. *I'm not even sure myself,* wrote the invisible hand. As Jo stared, mouth open, breath short, she noticed things. The writing was scratchy. Tiny flecks of ink spotted the page. And she could hear it: a scritchy sound. Not a ballpoint or gel pen, she thought, and was amazed at her calmness.

But with autumn here, the nights are getting longer and colder. More of the young ones are falling ill, and... In mid-sentence, the writing ended. Four lines of angular handwriting stared at her from the page. The last word glistened wetly a moment, then dulled as it dried. Then the writing faded, leaving the pages blank except for her own words.

Jo smacked the book closed. She leaned her head on her hands and massaged her eyes. *I've had a very long day. I'm very tired. This — thing in the book... It's not happening. My brain is completely scrambled and I'm seeing things. I'm hallucinating.*

After a moment she opened the journal again, touching just the edges of the pages with her fingertips. The only handwriting there was her own. She picked up her pen, moistened her dry lips, and cautiously put pen to paper. — *afraid of,* she finished. Then sat with pen poised. On the opposite page there was nothing — not a trace of ink. She held up the book sideways, to catch a slant of light. There was not even an impression to betray where that other hand had scratched those few phrases in blue ink. Which proved it never happened, right? She exhaled and wrote: *More tomorrow. I think I'm going nuts.* Then sat with the book open in front of her. She waited and watched for another ten minutes, but nothing else happened.

She put the journal away in the drawer of her bedside table, turned off the lamp and climbed into bed. The ceiling light switch was on the wall within reach. She reached over and pressed it, and the tiny lights slowly dimmed, letting the dark settle around her like a soft blanket.

The bed was Goldilocks, she thought with a smile, and made a mental note to write that in her journal next day. Goldilocks: not too soft, not too hard, just right. All the same, she tossed and turned a long time before sleep came.

Chapter 5

JO WOKE gasping for air. She sat up and pushed away the quilt and sat there breathing, reining in her gallopping heartbeat. The night was warm, yet she was shivering.

It was the same dream, the one she'd hoped would not follow her to this peaceful place. The deep, the dark, the cold. Her mad fight, pushing, pulling, fingers cramping, lungs screaming. The upward plunge to the surface, gulp air, down again. And again. And again.

Evan's arm, limp as weed. His eyes... oh, his eyes.

She rocked gently back and forth until the images faded and panic unhooked its claws. It took longer than usual. The dream had gained an extra layer of horror, a sense that she, like Evan, was trapped and drowning. That was new. She hoped it wasn't going to be a trend.

The glowing face of her digital clock said 1:16 a.m. She had closed the heavy dark drapes over the glass wall, leaving only the door uncovered. Its open pane let in musical liquid sounds and the long, slow sigh of wind in the trees. Perhaps it was the water sounds that had made the dream worse.

The open pane also let in a stagnant smell: pond water, mud, weeds. She wrinkled her nose. Time to shut that window. She put a foot out of bed. The stone floor was cold.

Someone cried out.

"Mel? What is it?"

The cry was not repeated. *Bad dream, somewhere. Seems I'm not the only one who gets nightmares.*

Pulling a terrycloth robe on over her thin nightshirt, she crossed to the glass wall and pulled aside the drapes. It was dark out there — the house lights were off — except for a white glow that radiated from the right. She slid open the glass door and the outside screen door and stepped out barefoot onto the terrace. A faint, cold light fingered out from behind the drapes that shrouded the windows of the room next door. Lew's room.

Something wrong? Jo wondered. Probably not. That glow must be a nightlight. But what a sickly-looking light to put in a kid's room! You'd think they could have found something more cheerful.

The cry came again. There were no words in it, but something in its tone made Jo spring forward and grab the handle of Lew's door. It was locked. She ran back into her room, through and out into the gallery. Something looked wrong here, but she was moving too fast to stop and work out what it was.

The cold white light seeped from under Lew's door and fanned across the floor to pick out the base of the opposite wall and door. Jo grabbed the doorknob, then snatched her hand away. The knob was cold as ice. Her hand came up chilled and wet.

She stared at her dripping palm a moment, then twisted the knob. As the door swung open the light faded, leaving the room dark. It took a moment for Jo's eyes to adjust. A nightlight plugged into the wall near the bed gave a soft rosy glow that lit up hardly anything. This room smelled of stagnant water too, even more strongly than hers. Odd, with the door locked and its window closed.

"Lew?" she called softly. A faint sound came from the bed.

He was huddled under the sheet, staring toward the window wall. His eyes were open wide, the whites showing all around the irises.

"Lew?" Jo knelt at the side of the bed nearest the window. "Lew!" She touched his hand. His eyes moved to focus on hers. Recognition lit his face and the terrified look softened.

"Bad dream?"

He moved his chin a centimeter.

She accepted that as a nod. "Okay now?"

His mouth folded down and he moved his chin the other way. *No.*

"Should I stay here for a bit?"

A nod. His fingers clutched weakly at her hand.

"All right, then." She got up and sat on the bed beside him. "I guess you're too old for a story, huh?"

No.

"Okay." Jo searched her memory for a story. "Well, here's one. I know it almost by heart, so I won't need the book. Stop me if it bores you. 'In a hole in the ground there lived a Hobbit…'"

Lew lasted nearly half an hour. When his eyes stopped fluttering open and his breathing grew slow and steady, Jo slid off the bed and went to the glass wall. She slid down the pane an inch to let in the soft, moist air and the endless music of flowing water and wind-stirred leaves. That should help him sleep, she thought.

But she felt a strange reluctance to leave the pane open. He had been staring in that direction when she came in. Staring as if something was there that he didn't dare take his eyes off. She shook her head at herself. There couldn't have been anything there. The door had been locked, the window closed. He'd had a bad dream, that was all.

All the same, she closed the window again. Maybe the air was a little too damp. It might not be good for him.

She stood looking around the room. Funny about that white light. What could have caused it? Certainly not the nightlight, with its dim pinkish glow. You'd almost think somebody had been in here carrying that icy white light, and had gone out by the terrace door. Which, of course, was impossible. Really, really weird, all of it.

And something else, Jo thought, as she stepped out into the gallery and noiselessly closed the door behind her. (Noting that the doorknob was no longer cold to the touch.) Something here had been different when she'd come running out of her room, but there hadn't been time then to think about it. It bothered her now.

She took a look back and forth. Small lights set low in the white walls gave enough light to find your way safely by night. They gleamed dully across the flagstones and traced the base of the white-painted parapet bordering the central well. More lights traced the curve of the spiral stairs.

Different. How was it different? What had she seen? Jo closed her eyes and tried to picture it. The cold light creeping from under Lew's door, the sheen of... not stone. A floor of dark wood, shiny, waxed. And... the opposite wall. Wall, not parapet. A wall with another door in it.

As if it hadn't been the same place at all.

FROM WHERE Calvin stood, by the south window of his room above the garage, if he pressed close to the screen he could see some of the trees across the stream from the house. A white glow was dying from the outer leaves, a glow that must be coming from the house. But from which room?

Now it was gone, and everything was black out there, except for the silver tracery of moonlight. He closed the curtain and turned on the light. No rest for him, not yet. The nightmare had found him after all, and now he had another of those images in his head. It would stay there, getting between him and sleep, until he did something to send it away.

Dream face: small, round, pale. Mop of fine, curly dark hair. So far, a bit like Lew. Eyes… couldn't see them. Didn't want to.

"Why do you keep coming back?" he asked the face. "Why are you in my dreams?"

He sat down on the bed and got out his supplies. As he set to work he wondered how he knew he wasn't insane. Most people would think of that explanation right away, he guessed, if strange faces kept cropping up in their dreams. But he'd always had a feeling they came from outside, they weren't the outpourings of a disordered brain. He trusted his gut instinct.

For years, he'd thought the nightmares gone. Thought he was cured. Then, a year ago, they'd started up again. A scattering at first. Maybe one a week. Then more and more often. This summer, early July, they'd been coming every night. Bad ones.

It looked like a pattern. There had to be a reason, right? He'd said nothing at all to his parents. Nothing even to Kyle, who liked to laugh but would not have laughed at him. And there was nobody else he could have told. He'd made up his mind he was going to figure out this thing himself. Figure it out and beat it. Until he did, he wasn't about to wreck anybody else's sleep by telling them.

And where better to figure things out than at Spinbrook House, so close to the place where it all started for him, all those years ago?

Chapter 6

IT WAS NINE o'clock by the time Jo dragged herself out of bed next morning and down the stairs to the kitchen. She was glad to find nobody had waited for her.

"We all get our own breakfast," said Melanie, from the big table in the middle of the room, where she was buttering toast and chasing it down with coffee. "Except Lew."

"And how's Lew this morning?" She fluffed his hair in passing. He gave her a small smile and went back to slowly chewing a spoonful of corn flakes Mel had popped in his mouth. Jo watched him out of the corner of her eye as she loaded frozen waffles into the toaster. It seemed to take all his strength just to chew and swallow.

"Bad night, Lew and me both," she said to Mel as she waited for the waffles to pop up.

"Lew?" Mel sat back. "What d'you mean? What happened?"

"Didn't you hear him call out?"

"Mm-mn." Mel shook her head. "I had a bad night too. Sometimes I wonder if there's such a thing as a good night in this place."

"Trouble sleeping?" Jo carried a plateful of waffles to the table and reached for the butter.

"I guess. I can't remember. I feel as if I've been climbing stairs all night. My legs are actually tired." Mel downed the last of her coffee and pushed back her chair. "Hey, d'you want a guide for the scenic tour? Hurry and finish, okay? I can't wait to get out of here."

"What scenic tour?"

"Oh... around." Mel waved an arm. "Aunt Frieda says I should show you, so you don't get lost."

"What about Lew?" She cut a piece of waffle as she spoke and held it out to him across the table on her fork, dripping with butter and syrup. He opened his mouth for it like a bird and crunched the piece, then gave Jo a real grin.

"Aha, I know the way to your heart! So, Lew — will you be my guide through the sinister cellars this morning?"

Lew's smile died. Mel dropped back onto her chair. "Cellars?"

"Which you didn't want me to see last night."

"It's a nice morning. The sun is shining! Wouldn't you rather be outside?"

"Now I'm really getting curious!"

Mel flung out her hands. "Oh, all right! It's one cellar, by the way, not cellars. You'd better see it now, or Aunt Frieda will insist on taking you down at some crappy hour of the night."

"You're trying to creep me out." Jo winked at Lew, but he didn't smile back. "C'mon, Lew, you coming?"

He shaped the word *no*.

"Will you be okay here by yourself for ten minutes?"

Yes.

Jo hesitated. She looked at Mel, who rolled her eyes and leaped up from the table. "Let's just get it over!"

THE CELLAR was at the bottom of the spiral staircase that connected the living room with the galleries. On the ground floor the stairs corkscrewed down into a circular well. The tiny lights along the baseboards continued here, so there was no need to flip a switch as Mel led the way down to the lower level. The stairs ended in a dim, concrete-walled space the size of a large closet, with a plain wooden door in the wall.

Mel stopped on the second stair from the bottom and flapped a hand at the door. "Go ahead. You're on your own."

Jo grinned at her. "Your secret fear! I got it! Cellars, right?"

"Not all cellars, no." She watched as Jo stepped down, pulled the door open and started in, then stopped.

"Where's the light switch?" Jo felt at the wall inside the door. The space ahead of her was so black it looked solid.

"There isn't one. They didn't run any wiring down here."

"Got a flashlight?" Jo backed out and closed the door.

"There's a little pen light in the kitchen. It's not much good." Mel started up the stairs again.

"I'll need something better than that. I'll ask Calvin."

"Jo…" Mel turned at the top of the stairs. "There's nothing *there*. Why don't you drop it?"

"Because you're making a mystery of it, and I'm stubborn."

Back on the ground floor, Jo crossed to the front door. As she stepped outside, Calvin walked past. On his shoulder he balanced a long metal pole with an outsized pair of scissors on one end. She caught up and fell into step beside him. "You look like you're on your way to chop down a giant beanstalk."

He sent her a flash of sky-blue eyes and the flicker of a smile. "It's for pruning trees."

"Would you have a good flashlight among your tools? That I could borrow? I want to check out the cellar."

He stopped and grounded the pole. "Why would you want to go down in the cellar?"

Jo was beginning to feel annoyed. "Oh, because people keep telling me not to. Why? Do they keep crocodiles down there?"

"Not the last time I looked." He gazed at her a moment longer, then nodded briefly. "I'll come with you."

"You don't have to. I don't need a bodyguard."

"Never thought you did." He stowed the pruning pole away in a long shed behind the garage and came out with a heavy rubber-sheathed flashlight. Then he followed Jo into the house and down the stairs to the cellar.

"BUT IT'S NOT a cellar at all!" Jo stared around at the rough, rocky walls and floor. "It's a cave!"

The ceiling nearly touched her hair. Calvin had to stoop. Close to the door, a layer of concrete had been poured to fill in the rougher places in the floor. Beyond the base of the hearthstone boulder, floor and roof curved down into darkness. The place where they met was out of sight beyond the curve.

"Looks like the perfect home for bats," Jo rubbed her bare arms. "Why is it so cold? It's like the inside of a refrigerator down here!" Mel was right. There was nothing to see. "Where do they keep the furnace and the water heater and laundry and so on?"

Calvin stuck his left thumb up at the ceiling. "Room beside the kitchen."

"Because of the damp, that figures." Rivulets trickled from four or five cracks in the walls. Some of the water ran into a wider crack that traced the base of the hearthstone boulder. The rest ran away into the darkness beyond the curve of the floor. The sound of flowing water echoed distantly, as if they stood on the banks of an underground river. You could smell it, too: a musty, closed-in, stony smell, not like the good smell of earth and rocks warming in the sun.

"Where does the water go?"

Calvin flashed the light into the far corner, where the darkness sucked it up. "Into the stream, I'd guess. Or into other caves below this one."

"You mean there are more holes like this?" She looked down at the cracked stone under her feet and pictured a nest of eroded limestone cavities, frail as bubbles clinging together in the bath. A secret darkness seemed to suck at her feet from below. She resisted the urge to back away toward the door. "That's... a bit disturbing." She forced a laugh. "Are we sure the whole place isn't going to collapse?"

"Nothing's sure, but I'm guessing it's safe enough." There was a smile in Calvin's voice. Did he guess how rattled she was? "I heard Mr. Stone say they had the cellar tested with radar a while back. There's at least one other cavity below here, but there's a lot of rock between."

Jo edged past him to the hearthstone boulder, which jutted out from the wall like a giant pilaster. She laid a hand on the granite and pulled it away with a gasp. "No wonder the house is cold! They've got their own natural chiller right below. Some hearthstone!"

"Well, this space hasn't seen the sun since… hm…" He scratched his chin. "Maybe never. You heard about those caves over near Collingwood where there's ice in mid-summer?"

"Yeah. This could be another one." She looked around again, hugging herself for warmth. A creepy, gloomy place, that was for sure. But not terrifying — not really. Mel had been afraid, really afraid, to come down here. Why?

"Seen enough?"

"You bet." Jo headed gladly for the door, close behind Calvin and his flashlight. The darkness flooded in at her back. She was a step short of the doorway and Calvin had passed through when something caught her eye, something that hadn't been there before. A pale gleam on the smooth wood of the door jamb: light reflected from behind.

She made a sound. Calvin looked back, and his eyes caught the gleam. "Jo," he said softly. "Come on." His hand closed around her wrist and he pulled.

"But, that light." She started to turn. Where's it — "

"Don't look!" Calvin yanked her through the door and slammed it shut with his elbow.

She twisted free. "Don't ever push me around like that again!"

"Yeah, okay. Sorry."

"You don't sound sorry!"

He jerked his head at the stairs. "You coming?"

"One sec." Cautiously, she opened the door. The cellar was solidly dark again. Yet for a moment she'd been sure she'd seen it, deep in the cellar, about where that crack around the base of the granite boulder would be: a fuzzy band of dead-white light. It made her think of the sickly glow she'd seen in Lew's room last night.

She closed the door with a bang and wished, for no reason that she could put into words, that it had a lock.

Chapter 7

"THIS IS A strange house," Jo said, as she walked into the kitchen.

"No kidding!" Mel, at the table, didn't look up from feeding Lew bits of buttered waffle.

"So, I didn't see any crocodiles down there, but there's something funny there all the same. I saw — "

She broke off. Frieda had come down the stairs, looking trim in a blue T-shirt and white shorts. "I'm snowed under today," she announced, beaming as if that was excellent news. "Got a big job to complete. If I don't surface in time to make dinner, I'm sure you two can cope. You'll find frozen entrees in the freezer, or, Jo, feel free to cook if that's what you like to do." She reached a mug down from a cupboard and poured coffee.

Frieda worked from a home office on the second floor. She seemed genuinely friendly, Jo thought: unflappable, too. *Go on, tell her! But tell her what?* There was so much to tell about last night, and this morning. So much, and at the same time so little. Guesses and feelings, mostly.

I need to tell somebody.

Coffee mug in hand, Frieda dropped a kiss on the top of Lew's head. "Melanie, will you stay with Lew until Mrs. Rhodes arrives?"

"Sure. He'll be fine with us."

"Of course he will." She headed out of the kitchen again with a wave and a smile.

"Mel, I..." Jo began.

"What?" Mel's face was stubbornly blank.

No, Jo thought. She's too scared, too young.

But I'm scared too. She thought of what she'd seen in the Cataract Room, and the writing — out of nowhere — in her diary last night, and the pale light in Lew's room. And her vision of the corridor as someplace different. And now, the ghostly light in the cellar.

Ghostly. Well, that was one explanation. If you believed in ghosts. *Never thought I did.*

"Back in a sec!" Jo ran out of the kitchen and up the stairs, taking the steps by twos to the second gallery level. "Frieda! Wait!" Frieda stopped in the doorway of her work room.

"Sorry — got a question. This house — has it changed much?"

"Changed?" Frieda blinked at her. "In what way?"

"You know: renovated. I'm wondering if that third-floor gallery ever looked different." She pointed up at the ceiling.

"How do you mean?"

"Well, was it ever enclosed? You know, walls on both sides? And was the floor up there ever wood, instead of stone?"

Frieda looked astonished. "My lord, no! Spinbrook House is unique, and it's very well known. It wouldn't pay to change it from the original. That's the reason we bought it, ten years ago. As an investment."

"So, the way it looks right now…"

"Is exactly the way the architect designed it. Now, I really must get down to work. We'll talk tonight!" Frieda flashed a smile and closed the door. Jo turned and went slowly down the stairs.

Mel had taken Lew outside. The mown turf in front of the house stretched for a few sunny metres to where a band of trees and shrubs screened the house from the county road. A gravelled driveway curled from the garage, passed the house and curved away into the trees. Lew's wheelchair was parked halfway between the front door and the garage, under a pergola overgrown with wild grape vines.

Mel sat on the short grass beside Lew's wheelchair. She hugged her tanned knees to her chest and lifted her face to the sun as if drinking it.

Jo dropped down beside her. "Mel, how old is the house?"

"It's, um..." She wrinkled her brows. "More than sixty years old, anyway. The date's cut into the stone over the door. Work it out."

Jo looked back over her shoulder. Yes, there it was. Spinbrook House was built sixty-three years ago. Not so very old, really. "Was there another house here before this one?"

"Another house? No clue. Can we stop talking about it *please?*"

Jo nudged her in the arm. "Is that your secret fear? The house?"

"No." Mel took a breath. "At least — not exactly."

"Want to talk about it?"

Mel shook her head.

"Okay. You know, seems like nobody around here likes to talk, except Frieda, and she's busy. Calvin's not exactly a gushing fountain either." Jo swivelled to face Lew. "But I bet you would talk, if you could. Right?"

He tilted his head a centimetre forward, his brown eyes serious.

There must be a way to talk with you. "Now, how can we do this?" She thought a minute, then knelt up, smiling. "Got it! How are you at spelling?"

Lew made a face as if he'd bitten a lemon.

Jo laughed. "Not so good? Me neither. Never mind, I'm a good guesser."

"What are you babbling about?" Mel squinted up.

"Communication. Is there a Scrabble game in the house?"

Chapter 8

AS MEL WALKED from the house, Scrabble box in hand, Calvin appeared from the direction of the shed. He carried a sloshing pail, a squeegee, and a roll of paper towels. He set to work cleaning the ground-floor glass after the briefest possible glance at the three on the lawn.

Jo unfolded the board and set it on the grass, then arranged an alphabet in the grid. "I'm going to touch each of these letters, one after the other," she said. "You can tell me which are the right ones, okay? Sometimes it's easier to spell things out than talk about them, anyway," she said cheerfully. "I had kind of a bad night last night, didn't you?" She glanced up. Lew was watching her closely. After a moment, he nodded.

"Maybe you're like me. I have weird dreams sometimes." She lifted the board and let it rest across the arms of his wheelchair. "How about you, Lew? Do you ever have any weird dreams?" *Keep it light, keep it fun. Don't scare him.*

Lew took a long, shaky breath, and nodded. *Oh-oh, he's already scared.*

"Lew, do you want to do this, really?" Mel asked. "You don't have to."

He stared at the board, then, with an obvious effort, nodded hard.

"Smart guy," Jo said. *Brave kid.* "Okay, here's the question." She hesitated, watching his face. "What was the thing you saw last night? The thing that scared you? Let's see if we can spell it out."

Lew's eyes darkened. He followed Jo's hand as it moved over the rows of tiles. She touched the A. No reaction from Lew. The B. Still no reaction. Slowly her finger moved along the rows of letters, stopping to tap each one. She began to wonder if he understood what she was doing, or if he'd decided not to play, or…

Lew made a soft noise. "Jo, stop," Mel said. "Stop there."

Jo's forefinger rested on the N.

"All right!" She grinned at him. "Now we're rolling. Next letter!"

Next was the E. Then R, S, and again E.

"This is starting to sound like something, anyway," Jo said, uncertainly.

"Nerse? That's not even a word."

Lew made a noise and moved his chin down.

"Wait a minute." Jo laughed. "Not nerse with an 'e'. Nurse with a 'u'! Is that it?" He nodded. "And is there more? What else can you tell us?"

Again she moved her fingers over the tiles and watched for his nod. Slowly the words took shape. N… O… T… D… R… E… M…

"Not drem," Jo said. "You mean, not dream. It wasn't a dream. It was real. Is that it?"

He nodded, then settled against his brace with a sigh.

"We've tired the kid out," Mel said. She tipped the Scrabble letters into the box, folded up the board, and carried the box back into the house. Jo followed her, stopping in the doorway to keep an eye on Lew.

"And what good was all that?" Mel demanded. "What does it mean?"

"The thing that scares him is a nurse."

"So, a bad dream about a nurse."

"He says it's not a dream."

Mel waved that away. "It can't be real. He doesn't have a night nurse, just a day nurse." She set the box down on a table in the hall and headed out the door again. "And here she comes. Mrs. Rhodes."

Gravel crunched. A red Camaro pulled up in front of the garage. The woman who slid from the driver's seat was sturdily built, middle-aged, and dressed in khaki pants and a bright yellow T-shirt.

"She doesn't look like a nurse," Jo said, as they crossed the lawn toward Lew. "Where's her uniform?"

"I asked her about that. She said she never wears her hospital gear for home visits. It reminds her kids — that's what she calls them — reminds them too much of needles and catheters and whatnot."

Even before they reached the pergola, Jo could tell that Lew wasn't afraid of this woman at all. His smile was brilliant. Mrs. Rhodes knelt in the grass beside the wheelchair and brushed a lock of hair back from his forehead. "You look a little down today," she said. "Let's see what we can do about that."

"He's in good hands," Mel murmured. "Hey, I've gotta get away from the house or I'll go totally bananas. You wanna come with?"

"Sure. What d'you have in mind?"

"For starters, let's go swimming! I know the perfect place."

"HERE?" JO STOOD on a rock at the water's edge and looked down at the glossy surface of the dark pool. "You want to swim here?"

"Why not? It's safe." Mel tweaked the strap of her tiny scarlet swimsuit. "Uncle Harold tested it with the pruning pole, one day. The pole couldn't reach bottom in the middle. There's no rocks to hit your head on and no weeds to get tangled in. Nothing but water. What could be better?"

"Yeah, just great," Jo muttered. She smoothed her new blue-and-white suit. "It doesn't look too clean, though. I mean, it's not... um, it's not clear."

"That's because it's in the shadow of the hill. Of course it's clean, it's only stream water! Come on!"

"Uh..." Jo breathed slowly, deeply, in the nose, out the mouth, the way Dr. Klein had taught her. And with each breath, her mantra: *I'm safe. I'm in control.*

"Okay, if you're chicken, I'll go first." Mel dove from the rock and pierced the surface like a knife slicing into jelly. Jo's heart stuttered, then beat on at double time. Mel had vanished, leaving nothing but a series of widening circular ripples. You'd think she'd been sucked down into a pool of ink.

Silence. Stillness. Nothing but the ripples, one after the other, lapping the rocks at Jo's feet, and then even they were gone. How long had it been since Mel went in? Three seconds... four... five... Jo's heartbeat pounded in her ears. She realized she was holding her breath. She remembered to breathe. In, out... Twelve seconds.... fifteen... still not a sign.... "Mel!" she gasped.

And gasped again as Mel's dark head broke the surface in the middle of the pool. She stroked to the south shore and climbed out on a flat rock, grinning victoriously, spraying water all around and pushing wet hair out of her eyes.

"It's fine!" she called. "A bit cold, that's all. How long was I under?"

"Long enough for me to have a heart attack!"

Mel laughed. "Your turn!"

"O-okay." Jo took a minute to work on her breathing. In, out. Her heart was still pounding. It took another couple of minutes to bring the beat back to normal. *Mel did it. It's perfectly safe. I can do this.*

"Hey!" Mel waved her hands crosswise over her head. "What are you waiting for? Christmas?"

"Give me a sec!"

"Oh-oh." Mel was staring at her. "I get it! This is your secret fear, isn't it? You're scared of the water. Can't swim?"

"Of course I'm not scared!" Jo snapped. "I'm a very good swimmer. I just... don't..."

"It is! That's your fear! Ha, you lose! Now you have to go in!"

With Mel jeering on the other side of the pool, sheer stupid embarrassment swamped Jo's fear. That, and a burst of resolution. Because Dr. Klein was right, life was full of the unexpected. Walk around any corner and she might see or hear something that would trigger memories of that terrible day on Nova Scotia's south shore. The day Evan tried to cure her phobia, her lifelong fear of dark water.

I can't live in a box for the rest of my life.

"All right, I'm going in!" Not giving herself time to ease in, she dove. She surfaced almost at once, spraying water from her hair. Treading water, she looked around. It was okay. It was absolutely okay. What had she been scared of?

The water was too cold for swimming, really, but it smelled fresh as the surrounding forest. Underfoot she felt no mud or rocks, no weed, no hungry fish come to nibble her toes. Nothing but water. Just like being in a swimming pool. She laughed back at Mel. Then, to prove to herself there was not a thing to be scared of, absolutely nothing at all, she upended like a duck and dove downward.

Holding her breath, she opened her eyes. It was colder down here. An icy current, distinct as if it flowed in its own channel, cut across her body. She wondered if it came from one of the rivulets in the cellar.

But it wasn't really dark. Instead it was dim and green. Her hands in front of her eyes looked bloodless. The surface glimmered not far above, a crinkled green-gold ceiling. She twisted to look down. A school of silver minnows fanned out beneath her feet. Below them, the green light faded into darkness.

Deeper still, at the farthest edge of the light, a pale shape moved. Not a fish. Something larger. It rose toward her.

Chapter 9

CALVIN DIDN'T MIND cleaning windows. It was a simple job, which made it perfect for thinking about complicated things, but it wasn't a thankless job. There was some satisfaction in washing the dust and bird poop off a sheet of glass, scouring off the occasional sticky blob of pine resin, leaving the window crystal-clear.

The part he didn't like was when he saw things in the glass. Things that were not his own reflection. It used to happen a lot. Not so much any more, and they didn't spook him like they used to. Or not usually.

He was squeegeeing a window on the west end of the house, near the garage, when another face frowned out at him where his own should be. It was a boy's face, maybe fifteen give or take a year, fair-haired, thin. He'd seen it before and always wondered why it looked so familiar. Yet he could never put a name to it.

"Who are you?" he asked, more casually than he felt.

"Never mind that. You got to get to the pool," the kid snapped. "Right now!"

"Oh, yeah?" Calvin slopped soapy water on the face and wiped at it with his squeegee. "Says who?"

The frowning young face was still there when he looked again. "Says me."

"Gimme a name, buddy."

"Look — the bad thing is down there, okay?"

"Like I don't know that."

"And that new girl? She's easy meat for it. She's in the pool! So hurry, willya!"

The squeegee hit the grass and bounced.

JO HAD NO breath left. She rose and surfaced, gulping air.

"Okay, okay!" Mel called. "That's enough. I take it back, you're not scared."

"Something's down there." Jo's heart was pounding so hard she could barely breathe. But she had something to prove — to herself, not to Mel. "I'll take another look."

"No!" Not Mel's voice. Jo swirled around in the water. Calvin stood on the bank nearest the house. "Get out of there!" he yelled.

"Why?" she yelled back.

"Just get out! Now! There's danger!"

"Oh, Calvin." Mel laughed across the water. "What could possibly be dangerous here?"

He ignored her. "Jo — look at the water. Look at the water!"

She looked. She floated in the centre of the pool. Her small movements sent a few ripples across the dark surface, but that was all. There was nothing... No, there was something. A line of yellowish-white foam turned in a circle just beyond arm's length. A bubble rose and broke within the circle. There was a swampy smell.

"It's nothing," Jo called. "Only some foam."

But fear nibbled at her heart. Where had she seen a foam circle like that, not long ago? A slow, lazily spinning circle. Oh... right... Under the Cataract Room, last night. A moment or two before that dead-looking hand plastered itself against the glass.

Means nothing, she told herself. I'm cold and tired, that's all. There's nothing to be afraid of. She headed for the far shore, swimming strongly and smoothly, not in a panic, careful not to thrash.

Two strokes, and Mel, standing on her rock, was nearer. Two

more strokes, and something closed around Jo's right ankle and pulled. She screamed and at the same moment Calvin shouted.

Jo choked as her head went under. She clawed at her ankle. Something cold and strong and smooth was there, something that would not let go. It pulled and pulled. It was her childhood nightmare come to life. Something lurking in dark water. Something that waited there to grab and pull her down. But this was no dream, no imagined horror, it was real.

Desperately holding her breath, she kicked and flailed. It held on. It pulled. Darkness closed in. Her chest hurt. One more second and she would have to open her mouth and draw breath, and then...

And then the pull was gone. Jo shot upward and broke through the surface side by side with Calvin. She splashed through the water and struggled onto the rocks. Mel tugged her the last of the way out and they collapsed in a wet heap together.

"What was it?" Mel demanded.

"Dunno." Still gasping, Jo crawled away from the water's edge.

"You went down like — like something pulled you!" Mel's voice ratcheted up.

Jo sat down and rubbed her ankle. It was cold and numb. "Don't... don't be silly."

Calvin pushed dripping hair off his face. He had gone in with all his clothes on, including his sneakers. He stood up, streams running off him, and scowled down at her. "How's your foot?"

"Hurts a bit." She propped it in front of her and turned it this way and that, wiggling the toes.

"Ugh," Mel said.

A dead-white band almost completely circled Jo's right ankle. Over the ankle bone, where the ends of the band almost met, five small cuts broke the skin. The mark was icy to the touch.

Jo pulled her knees up and cinched her arms around them and tried to breathe. Couldn't. Shivers were shaking her to pieces. She rocked back and forth, eyes tight shut, couldn't stop shaking. Saw that pale shape again. That shape, and then Evan, pale in the dark water, his hands drifting. *Oh help me —*

Strong arms went around her, covering her own arms, holding her together. He rocked with her and held her until she knew she was not going to fly into pieces after all. The shivering stopped. Calvin sat back. "Okay now?"

"Y... yeah. Thanks." She cleared her throat. "Looks repulsive, doesn't it? Some weed caught me, I guess. I, I freaked."

"Weed!" He made a scornful noise.

"Fish, then." Jo went to work, massaging warmth and colour back into her ankle. It had to be a fish that attacked her. Not a minnow. A largish fish with sharp teeth. It could not be... what it looked like. She rubbed harder.

"Some fish," Calvin said, almost gently. "Tell me you won't go back in."

"Oh, I won't." She looked up at him and forced a smile. "Ever."

"Good." He looked past her to Mel. "You'll talk to your aunt about sending the kid away, right?"

"Lew? Send him away? Why?"

"Don't pretend you don't know what I'm talking about." He stood up. "If you don't say something today, I will."

"Aunt Frieda won't like that."

"So let her fire me." Calvin turned, still dripping, and started back across the stepping stones.

"Wait!" Jo called after him. But he didn't wait, and a minute later he had vanished into the trees on the other side of the stream.

Chapter 10

"WHAT DID HE mean?" Jo stayed close behind Mel as they crossed the stepping stones, and wished she would move faster. She itched to get away from this place. "What he said about Lew. What do you both know that I don't know?"

"Calvin's strange," Mel said breathlessly, as she jumped from the last rock to the shore. "If you want a mystery, ask him what's in that room of his above the garage."

Jo let herself be diverted. "How do you there's anything mysterious there at all?"

"Because he always keeps it locked up. Ask him what he keeps there besides the Crown Jewels."

"His privacy, I'd guess," Jo said. She caught at Mel's arm and stopped her. They faced each other on the path. "Mel, I'm serious. There's something really strange going on."

"Nothing's going on!"

"No? So why are you so scared of that cellar? And why wouldn't you go into the Cataract Room last night?"

Mel threw her towel over her head and rubbed at her hair. She started up the path again toward the house. "You were wrong to come here," she said, muffled. "The place is making you more crazy, not less."

"Mel!" Jo stepped in front of her. "Look at me!" Mel's face emerged warily from the towel. "I've seen... or felt... some things I can't explain. Here at Spinbrook House. What happened in the pool — that's just one thing. There've been more. I haven't worked out why this is happening. But I'm not going to pretend it isn't happening."

Mel took a deep breath and let it out slowly. "Me too."

"Then what's — "

"I'll go to bits if I talk about it. Don't ask me!" Mel buried her face in the towel again. Her hands were shaking.

"Okay. But remember I'm here when you're ready to talk. Even if it's the middle of the night. Because when you do, I'll have some things to tell you, too."

"Nightmares," Mel muttered.

"I wish."

MEL WAS STILL determined to colour the day normal, so they put on sneakers, stuffed T-shirts and tubes of sunblock into a bag, packed a picnic lunch and walked to the far side of MacPhee, where the stream turned an old quarry into a perfect natural swimming pool. The water, Jo was happy to see, was so clear you could see every fragment of gravel on the bottom.

They splashed and swam and dove for pretty stones until they were tired, then lay on the hot, smooth rocks and soaked up the sunshine. Ate their sandwiches, washed down with cans of sweet cider. Pulled on tees over their still-damp swimsuits. Walked to a berry farm a mile down the highway and picked a pint of strawberries. Washed the berries in the stream and walked back along the highway, eating them off the stems. They bought ice cream cones at the general store and sat on the wooden bench in the afternoon sun to eat them and watch the slow life of the village amble past.

"Feeling sane now?" Mel asked, as Jo swallowed the last bite of waffle cone and licked smears of chocolate ice cream off her fingers.

"Marginally. You?"

"I'm awesome! Only, with all we're eating, I'm going to gain a ton."

"You, Grasshopper?" Jo laughed. "Me, maybe. Let's walk it off!"

With flasks of water and packages of nuts-and-raisins in their packs, they explored the countryside west of MacPhee. The village was located close to the Corduroy Hills conservation area, a landscape of forest-choked ravines and foaming brooks and cave-riddled limestone cliffs.

On the edge of the forest they came upon what Jo at first thought was a garden inside a wrought-iron fence, until she saw the rows and rows of upright stone slabs among neatly kept plots of flowers and shrubs. "This must be the local cemetery. Let's go in." She looked along the fence for the entrance.

"Are you crazy?" Mel grabbed her arm. "No!"

"Why not?"

"I hate cemeteries!" Mel turned her back on the fence.

"You kidding? They're interesting! Peaceful, historic..."

"Depressing!"

Mel wrapped her arms around herself and gripped her biceps with white-knuckled hands. Jo opened her mouth to argue, then closed it again. As she turned to follow Mel along the dirt path into the woods, her sneaker brushed smooth rock. She looked down, then knelt to push the long grass aside. "Hey, look at this!"

It was a gravestone set flat in the earth. Old and worn, but you could still trace the words on it. "Ellen Quinn," Jo read aloud. "1875 – 1897. Gosh, she was only twenty-two. A year younger than me. That's so sad."

"Jo, will you get away from there?"

"Wait, there's another bit, under the dates. It says, 'May God forgive her.'" She looked up at Mel. "Why would they put that?"

Standing up, she frowned down at the stone. "And why is it out here, outside the fence? Why isn't it in with the others?"

"Jo, if you don't come on right now, I'm leaving you here."

"Oh, all right!"

They walked the sun out of the sky. Jo knew what Mel was doing: deliberately wearing them both out. Making them both so tired they would fall asleep and stay asleep all night. She was all for that.

At the back of Mel's eyes, even when she laughed, Jo saw a shadow. It's something that happens at night, she thought. That's what's got Mel so scared. Something at night. And she doesn't want to be awake to see it.

Chapter 11

AS THEY TRUDGED up the drive from the highway in the level golden light of sunset, tired and dusty, Jo saw Calvin cross the lawn and disappear around the corner of the house.

"There's a guy I want to talk to," she said.

Mel raised eyebrows at her. "Need backup?"

"Alone would be better. I think then he'd be more likely to talk."

"Be my guest. I've never got more than two sentences in a row out of him. Here, I'll take your bag." Mel grabbed it and headed for the front door.

The garage was a small detached building past the west end of the house, near the crest of the hill above the stream. Jo climbed a narrow flight of wooden stairs on the west side to a small landing and knocked on the door. After a moment it opened. Calvin stared at her a moment with no expression on his face, then stepped out and closed the door behind him.

As the door closed she looked past him into the dark interior. She would have stepped backward if there had been room on the tiny landing. She gripped the wooden railing and held on tight. "Who's that in there?"

"Nobody's in there."

"Maybe I should've said what, not who." She let go her grip on the railing, but still felt shaken. "I saw a face…"

"There's a mirror on my closet door. Maybe you saw your reflection."

She studied him suspiciously, but his tight mouth didn't betray even a hint of a smile. "I don't look like that, thanks very much. If I did, I'd wear a bag over my head."

"Scared you?"

"Well... yeah." She waited. He slid his hands into his pockets and rocked gently, heel-to-toe. She sighed. "You're not going to explain, are you?"

His eyes went bluer when he smiled. He dipped his head at the stairs and she went down ahead of him. "I didn't come here to poke my nose in," she said over her shoulder.

"No, eh?"

"Okay, I did, but not only for that. I came to say thank you."

"For what?"

"For this morning. The pool."

From the bottom of the stairs they started toward the house, slowly, scuffing through the grass. I like this, Jo thought with surprise. The grass was soft underfoot and had that fresh, bright, newly mown smell. The evening sun warmed her neck. And there was something in Calvin's quiet company that made her feel fully alive, and — in spite of all the trouble tingling at her nerve-endings — happy.

"By the way," she said, "what made you come down to the pool just then? Are you psychic?"

"You mean, do I see things?" He laughed, but he didn't sound amused. And he didn't answer the question. "Good thing I did come by. Left to Mel, that might've been the end of you."

"The end of me? From a fish bite?" Her laugh didn't sound amused either, even to her.

He gave her a sideways smile and shook his head. That's the place to drop it, Jo told herself. Do I really want to know more? Yes, I do.

"Calvin, what — what did you see down there?"

"Nothing I'd swear to. It was too dark."

"But you felt something?"

"Yes." His voice was very soft.

"What did you do?"

"Fought. Like you were doing." He held out his right arm. "Got marked, like you."

It was still light enough to see the white mark circling his wrist. She didn't need to look at her ankle to know the white band and the five sharp marks were still there. The band was not as cold as it had been that morning, but she could still feel it.

"It looks like… like…" She swallowed. "Well, not a fish bite."

"It looks like the print of a hand."

She couldn't deny it, but she didn't want to admit it, either. Fear was already digging its claws in. She focused on breathing evenly. They strolled across the lawn in front of the house. Long shadows striped the grass. Jo kept looking into the woods, watching for pale shapes.

The big windows of the house lit up, one after the other. She caught sight of Lewis, in his wheelchair, looking out from the living room. She waved at him. He smiled back. "Such a sweet kid," she said. "And so... so vulnerable."

She looked up at Calvin, who was watching Lew with dusk-darkened eyes. Calvin, who had fought for her. Gone down into the dark, knowing there was danger, maybe knowing what kind of danger, and fought to free her. And he didn't even know her. And she didn't know him. And she wanted to.

"Hey. I, um, I'm going to tell you something crazy."

"Shoot." He looked mildly interested.

"Something happened last night in the Cataract Room." She told him about the hand under the glass floor. "And later there was this strange white light in Lew's room. I don't know where it came from. It just came, then faded. Kind of like the light in the cellar." She waited, but he said nothing and looked nothing. "And today, Lew... he seemed to me..."

Calvin nodded, his eyes on the window where Lew was still sitting, watching them. "He's been getting weaker all summer, a little bit more every day. But this last week, he's been getting worse, faster."

"Then why don't his parents take him away? Why isn't he in the hospital? It's not like they don't care."

On the other side of the window, Frieda stopped beside Lew and tenderly smoothed back his hair.

"They don't think about it," Calvin said. "They don't see it. I don't think they can."

"But why not, when it's so obvious to you and me and Mel?"

"I think something stops them."

Jo clenched her fists. "What's this *something*? I don't understand!"

"Why should you need to? You don't live here, you can go away. You can be safe."

"You think so?" She scowled up at him. "When there's Lew, and Mel — I can't run out on them. I hardly know them, yet it would be... well... weaselly. Besides, I...." She broke off, folding herself around her secret core of pain.

He studied her face, then shook his head, as if to deny the whole subject. "It's getting dark. Better get inside." He started toward the garage, but she took hold of his wrist.

"Why do you stay? You don't have any friends or relatives here. This is only a job for you."

"It's not only a job."

"No? Then what?"

"Unfinished business." He turned away.

WHEN HE TURNED at the corner of the garage and looked back, she was standing on the lawn near the front door, staring after him. As if embarrassed to be caught gazing, she sketched a wave and darted into the house.

The sun was down and a white mist was wisping through the trees from the ravine, bringing the smell of wet stone and earth. He shivered and went up the stairs by twos. Inside his one-room flat, he made sure the door was locked. Not that that would make much difference if a nightmare decided to hunt him down.

There was time for a little work — his real work — before he set off on his evening walk.

Chapter 12

JO'S GEL PEN scurried across a fresh page in her journal. *So that's how my day went. Sunshine and near-drowning, ice cream and graveyards. I'd planned to do some calm, quiet thinking, to start working out what's going on with me, try to pry off this horror that's got its claws in me — but there was no time. Fresh horrors pushed the old ones aside. I don't know if that's good or bad.*

What's the matter with this house, that it breeds bad dreams? Lew gets them, and I think Mel does too, and mine was worse than usual last night. Calvin's right, I have no reason to stay. But if I run, I'll be sabotaging my healing. I'm almost certain what's happening to me now — or what I think I'm seeing and feeling — no, what I am seeing and feeling — is worse because of the PTSD. Whatever it is, I have to face it, and get the better of it, or I may never get better, and...

The pen dropped from her hand and rolled across the table. She let it fall to the floor. There it was again, the scratchy writing, working its spiky blue way across the opposite page with no hand to hold the pen. *...nightmares,* it began. *More of us are getting them. And worse than nightmares, I'm dead sure. Last night I got up and the door handle was cold as ice, and it was wet. Marie believes, but the others only want to curl up in their beds and pretend it isn't happening. I have got to convince them...*

"What the hell is going on?" Jo demanded. She kept her eyes on the journal. The writing paused, as if the writer had heard a noise and looked over his or her shoulder. Then it went on. *...to talk, to admit* *the truth. There is strength in numbers. But not unless we can agree to work together.*

"Who are you?"

The invisible writer ignored her. *I fear most for the young ones. This morning little Esther was too weak to leave her bed. Marie tried to stay with her last night, but the Sisters sent her off, saying she would only be in the way.*

Jo scooped her gel pen off the floor and attacked her side of the journal. *What's going on?* she scrawled. *Who are you?*

The scratchy writing stopped with a scatter of blue drops. Jo almost heard the caught breath. *Who...* The writing faded.

Jo dropped her pen again, dashed out to the gallery, and burst into Mel's room. Mel was lying on the bed with an old-model CD player on her stomach and giant headphones on her head. Jo yanked the headphones off. "You've got to see this!"

"What happened?" Mel sat up.

"Just come!"

Mel grumbled, but allowed herself to be dragged next door. As she watched impatiently, Jo wrote and waited and wrote and waited for another fifteen minutes. The opposite page stayed blank.

"Wow, what a huge waste of my time." Mel slammed out of the room.

"Wouldn't you know it," Jo said bitterly. She flipped to the last quarter of the journal and wrote down every word that the invisible pen had written, yesterday and today, so far as she could recall. She left the book invitingly open on the table for another hour, while she sat beside it, yawning. Nothing else happened.

She went to bed and fell asleep almost as soon as her head touched the pillow.

CALVIN WOKE with a yell. For a second or two he fought with the clinging sheets. Then realized where he was. In his bed. Not drowning. He lay back, sweating.

He'd pounded the pavement for a full hour that evening, and it hadn't done him any good. Might as well save my energy, he thought. In fact, it was possible he'd been making things worse. Exhausting himself, maybe, was making it that much harder to fight free of the dream.

What time was it? He fumbled for his alarm clock on the bedside table and pressed the backlight button. It was 2:15. He was wide awake, no point in lying back. He threw off the sweaty sheets, pulled on the jeans and tee that were hanging over the end of the bed and a pair of sneakers from under it, unbolted his door, and stepped out into the night.

He wasn't sure, himself, what he was up to. He just had a strong feeling that it was a good idea to... well, keep an eye on things. He thought of Jo, and Lew, and Mel, all with their rooms right over the ravine. All sleeping.

Crossing the moon-silvered lawn to the house, he looked into the ground-floor windows. Nothing moved in there, so far as he could tell.... No, wait. From here at the front of the house he could see all the way through to the living room. The spiral stairs were outlined by the soft glow of their floor-level lights. Something moved on the stairs leading up from the cellar. Someone climbed up from below. The head turned, features caught the light. Then the figure climbed on upward.

"If that's who it looks like," Calvin muttered, "then it's okay... I guess. But what would she be doing in the cellar? At this hour of the night? In the dark?"

"*If* that's who it looks like." His reflection seemed to repeat that, skeptically. Or was it the face that formed in front of his image in the glass that spoke? The face of a flaxen-haired boy, a mere kid, teasingly familiar.

"You again! Who are you?" Calvin demanded.

"Never mind that, something's happening!"

"And who are you to be telling me?"

"Will you stop mucking around and get in there!"

"Wait a minute, you look sort of like...."

"Just go!" The image flickered like an old-time film and vanished.

Calvin scrubbed at his head with both hands. "This is nuts!"

He wavered. He wanted to sit down and give some thought to what it meant, his being visited by a reflected face that looked — admit it — a lot like his own, when he'd been that age, fifteen or sixteen or so. But why the hell would the image of his younger self be following and nagging him like this?

But something even more troubling was in the air. He needed to get inside, scope it out. He knew where to find the spare key to the front door. Mrs. Stone had shown him where to look, in case some emergency came up. But was this an emergency? Maybe it was, but would Mrs. Stone see it that way? He doubted she would like him to be prowling around her house in the middle of the night, for no reason that would make sense to her, and he wouldn't blame her for getting mad about it.

On impulse, he turned and walked past the house to the west, slipped through the gap between the house and the garage, and stood on the brow of the hill above the stream. From here he had a good view of the windows on the south side, above the Cataract Room. Behind the iron railings of the second- and third-floor terraces, the house was a dark, glinting glass wall.

Then... Calvin's stomach went cold. There it was again, that sickly white glow, exactly like last night. It was on the third floor, coming from one of the bedrooms.

He whirled and ran.

Chapter 13

JO WOKE suddenly from dreams of struggle, of water, dreams that faded and left her dazed and sweating in the dark. It was 2:15 a.m. by her digital clock. Still muzzy with sleep, she groped her way out of the room and along the gallery, past Mel's door, to the bathroom. The small lights along the base of the wall lit her way clearly.

A few minutes later she came out of the bathroom and closed the door softly behind her. Then looked up, and froze with her hand on the knob. The gallery had changed again.

The little lights were gone, and so was the balustrade that guarded the central well. Where the gallery had been, a long corridor stretched away with, on both sides, closed doors set in heavy mouldings. She was alone. The floor was polished dark wood, with a strip of brownish carpet running along the centre. Small lamps with frosted glass shades were fixed to the walls. Jo peered at the one closest to her head. The glass was etched with morning glories.

When she looked along the corridor again, it was no longer deserted. Her heart jumped into her throat. Someone stood at the far end. She — it looked like a woman — was facing the last door on the left, one hand on the doorknob. A slender woman dressed in long, narrow clothing, clothing so white that it glowed in the dimness.

The face was turned away, and it was impossible to see exactly what the person was wearing — hard to pick out any detail — but Jo felt she would know who this was if only she could see the face.

She also felt, very strongly, that she had to stop the woman from opening that door and going in. It was Lew's door. Jo knew that was so even though the place looked all wrong.

She started along the hall. It was strangely hard to move, the way it sometimes is in dreams. Step by slow step, she forced her feet to carry her toward the glowing figure. *I should call out. I should get her attention. Tell her to stop.*

But the face was still turned away, and Jo knew, in the pit of her stomach, that she did not want the woman to turn and look at her. She did not want to see that face. More important, she didn't want it to see her.

But I have to stop her!

Slowly, slowly, Jo pushed on toward the end of the corridor. Not quite so slowly the doorknob turned, the door opened, the woman passed inside, the door closed, all in utter silence. A sickly greenish-white light seeped from beneath the door.

A low cry broke the silence. *Lew!* The noise released Jo's feet. She covered the last couple of yards at a dash. The doorknob was wet and icy cold. She flung open the door and stood staring.

The room looked different, too. It was much bigger than Lew's room, for one thing. There were two rows of narrow beds with metal frames and white covers, each with a small shape huddled in it, perhaps twelve beds in all. Some of the shapes stirred. Beside each bed was a little white cupboard and an oval of braided mat.

Then everything blurred, as if her eyes were a slide projector, and one slide had been whisked away and another slipped into place. Now she was looking at a smaller room with a flagstone floor and one big bed. There was no sign of the slender woman. The silver light shone from the bed for a moment, then faded as if the moon had gone behind clouds. The room smelled of pond water and wet earth.

"Lew?" Jo whispered. He whimpered, the sound almost too faint to hear. When she crossed the room and looked at him closely, his eyes were open and staring, his breathing shallow. He looked toward the window, not at Jo. "Lew!" He didn't seem to hear.

At a footstep behind her she spun around, hands instinctively flying up. Then she sagged. "You! What are you doing here?"

Calvin stood at the foot of the bed. "What are you doing here?"

"I asked you first."

"Thought I saw a light," he said carefully. "It looked, um, funny."

"Me too." She looked meaningfully at Lew. This was no place to be talking about what she'd seen in the corridor. "Everything's okay now."

Calvin frowned. "Sure?"

"Totally. We'll talk tomorrow, okay?"

He nodded slowly, glanced at the window, frowned at her again, and left.

A minute or two later the door opened again and Mel put her head in. "What happened?" she whispered.

"Nothing. Everything's okay."

Mel let out a sigh of relief. "I was worried about...."

"No need." *Talk tomorrow,* Jo mouthed. Mel nodded and closed the door.

Jo sat with Lew for two hours, telling stories and singing softly, until his breathing deepened. For another hour and a half she sat on the quilt beside him, her head against the padded headboard, drowsing and yanking herself awake over and over, while he slept. Then, as the sky beyond the terrace began to pale, she tiptoed away to her own room.

Chapter 14

LEW HAD NO appetite at breakfast. He even refused a bite of waffle dripping with butter and syrup.

His mother clucked over him. "You should eat! We need to get some meat on those bones!"

"He's not strong enough," Jo said. "Look, he can hardly even chew."

Frieda looked at him with puzzled eyes. "Well, that won't do." She picked up the spoon and began feeding him corn flakes. After two mouthfuls he closed his mouth and his eyes and kept them closed.

Mel and Jo exchanged a look. They had talked before breakfast about the events of the night before. Mel cleared her throat. "Maybe if you take him away, Aunt Frieda. Maybe that would help."

"Away?"

"Right," Jo chimed in. "I bet he'd get better real fast if — well, if you took him somewhere like — well, like Florida."

"Florida! In August?" Lew's mother stared. "Why on earth?"

"Not Florida, then. Vancouver. Winnipeg." Jo waved her hands. "A complete change of scene. It would do Lew good to get away, don't you think?"

Frieda shook her head. "Lew's perfectly fine here. Besides, we've only lived here a year."

"A year?" Jo met Mel's shadowed eyes. "But I thought — didn't you say you've had the house for ten years?"

"That's right. We held it as an investment for a long time before we realized it wasn't the kind of house to sell easily. And then there was some trouble with Harold's business and we couldn't afford two houses, so we sold the one in Toronto and moved here." Frieda began to clear the breakfast dishes to the sink.

"And you moved in a year ago?" Jo jumped out of her chair and followed her across the room. "But isn't that when Lew started getting sick?"

"Well, yes, but–"

"Don't you see? That proves it! This house is bad for him!"

Frieda opened her eyes wide. "Bad for him? How could that be? It's a very well-built house."

"Maybe it's — um..." Jo scooped air with her hands, grasping for anything plausible. "Something in the soil. Or in the stream. Pollution."

"Heavy metals," Mel put in.

"Now, that's silly!" Frieda tapped Mel playfully on the nose. "Look at me. I'm fine, and I spend almost every day in the house."

"But–" Jo began.

"Mel, you'll do the dishes, all right? And would you please keep an eye on Lew until Mrs. Rhodes arrives?" She waved a hand, breezed out of the kitchen and up the stairs.

"You see?" Mel said. "Rose-coloured glasses."

"What's wrong with her?"

"No clue."

Lew opened his eyes and looked at Jo. *Uh-oh.* She tried to recall what she'd been saying. Had she frightened him?

Then she got a good look at his face. He might have been gazing up at her from the bottom of a well. *Help me,* his eyes were saying.

He knew. Whatever was going on, he knew. She touched his hand. "I'll help," she whispered. "I'll do my best. I promise."

A car horn beeped outside. "There's Mrs. Rhodes," Mel said.

"The nurse! Right! We'll tell her." Jo hurried through the living room and out the front door. Mel followed her.

"Tell her what?" She looked back at the kitchen and lowered her voice. "That the house is killing Lew?"

"Not the house." Jo held her eyes. "Something in the house."

Mel looked away. "Right. That'll go over real well."

"We have to try, don't we? Or are you just going to…" She remembered something the invisible writer had said. "…curl up and pretend it isn't happening?"

Still, Mel had a point. By the time Mrs. Rhodes had reached the door, radiating determined good cheer, Jo had changed her mind. "Come and see Lew," she said.

He was still in the kitchen, slumped in his brace. His eyes flickered when they trooped in, but he had no smile for his nurse this morning. She sat on a chair beside him, looked him over carefully and checked his pulse. Then jumped up and climbed the stairs to the second floor, not quite running.

Ten minutes later she came down again, more slowly. "Your aunt seems rather preoccupied," she said to Mel. "I had a lot of trouble getting her to listen to me."

"She gets like that when she's working."

"I'm calling Dr. Bliss."

"Finally!" Jo murmured, as Mrs. Rhodes left the kitchen, tapping on her phone. She drained the last of her coffee and set the mug down hard. "We need a computer. I don't suppose we could get at Frieda's machine today. How about Calvin, does he have one?"

"He could have the Large Hadron Collider in that flat for all I know."

"Stay with Lew." Jo was out of the kitchen as she spoke. She found Calvin on his knees at the edge of a rose border, cutting dead-heads and tossing them in a bucket. No, Calvin did not have a computer. Couldn't afford one.

He sat back on his heels. "Why?"

"I need to find out if there was a building here before Spinbrook House."

"Any special reason?"

"Um..." It was going to sound crazy. But then Calvin seemed to have a wide tolerance for craziness. "I, um, I think I may have seen it last night. Some of it."

"Cool." He nodded as if this was only to be expected. "My buddy Kyle has a laptop he'd let me use. But he takes it with him to college in Owen Sound, and that's where he is today. You'd have to wait till tomorrow."

Jo glanced back at the house, and knew Calvin had followed her glance. "Tomorrow may be too late. I need to find a library."

Chapter 15

"ROAD TRIP! Yes!" Mel dropped the last dish into the draining rack. "Toronto! Malls! Civilization!"

"Probably not Toronto. We'll need to ask Frieda if we can borrow the car, and — "

"And I'll drive," Calvin said.

"Leave it to me!" Mel ran up the stairs.

"You don't need to do this," Jo said. "I can drive."

"I want to do this." He pulled up a tight smile. "If I don't I'll spend the day chewing my nails."

Two minutes later Mel was down again, purse swinging from her shoulder. "Go get your bag! Aunt Frieda says yes, take the car. And she wants me to buy a printer cartridge while we're in town. I have the model number written down."

As they drove through MacPhee, Calvin detoured down a side street and stopped in front of a small house with an enormous front yard. "Won't be long," he said.

Jo watched him disappear inside, noting that he did not knock or ring. "This must be where his family lives. Wow, look at that yard!" The front walk ran to the door between two gardens. On the left the yard was planted with tomatoes, lettuce, cantaloupes and beans. The other half of the yard was a storm of colour, more flowers than Jo had ever seen together in one place before.

"Love it," Mel said. She leaned forward from the back seat, eyes bright, dark hair lit to auburn by the morning sun. She caught Jo's questioning look. "Don't you feel it? The farther you get from Spinbrook House, the better you feel. It's like huge weights off my shoulders."

"Yes." Jo nodded slowly. "I feel it." Even the breeze, scented with all the flowers of the Ransom garden, seemed happier, more vibrant. Jo felt glad to be alive. Then she thought of Lew, sitting in his wheelchair in Spinbrook House with darkness in his eyes, and her heart went leaden with fear and guilt.

Okay, but we're going to do something about that. I promised him, didn't I?

Calvin waved goodbye to someone inside as he left the house. He slid behind the wheel, handed Jo a small, round object, and started the engine. "We can borrow that for a few hours if we're careful not to lose it."

Jo held it up so Mel could see it too. It was a brightly polished silver medal about an inch across, hung on a faded red ribbon. One side showed an open book surrounded by the words *For Proficiency in Mathematics — Jeremy Ransom — 1923.* The other side showed a flying dove and the words, *Sisters of St. Innocent.*

"What's this for?" Jo asked.

"I'll explain later," Calvin said. "After you explain why you think there was anything there before Spinbrook House."

"Okay, then." As they sped southeast along Highway 10, she described what she'd seen upstairs on her first two nights in the house. How the third-floor gallery had turned into another, older place. How writing had appeared in her journal: somebody else's writing, from — she'd swear — another time, if not another place. Mel, who had heard about the journal but not the vision of the corridor, sank down in the back seat and wrapped her arms around herself. Calvin kept his eyes on the road.

"That's all I know," Jo finished. "And don't tell me I've been seeing things. I know I'm seeing things. I just don't know why I'm seeing them." She had been congratulating herself on how calm she was about all this, but now she realized her right hand hurt. She opened it and found she had squeezed the medal so tight it had left a deep, curved groove across her palm.

"Unless you're hallucinating." Mel kicked the back of the seat.

"I guess that's possible," Jo said. "But I don't think so. I think these things are real."

"How about you, Mel?" Calvin asked casually. Jo saw his eyes dart to the rear-view mirror. He was watching Melanie. "You have any midnight adventures?"

"Me? Never." She sank as far down as her seatbelt would allow.

"Know what I think?" Jo wiped her palm on her shorts. "I think all this is connected with whatever is happening to Lew. I think s—something horrible is there, in Spinbrook House, or... or close by."

"The pool." Calvin fixed his eyes on the road. They were nearing the town of Burfast, and traffic was picking up.

"Right. But I think — just possibly — something else is there too. Someone, I mean. Someone not horrible. Who went through this, or something like it, before us. The person who keeps writing in my journal. Who might help, maybe." She added, "Okay, your turn. What's this medal?"

Calvin slowed down as Highway 10 became a street bordered by small shops and big, spreading trees. Mel stared glumly out the window. "Civilization, yeah, right," she muttered.

"That medal belonged to my great-grandfather," Calvin said at last. "That's how I know there was a building on that spot before Spinbrook House. It was an orphanage run by the Sisters of St. Innocent. He was one of the orphans. It burned down about 90 years ago."

"Orphanage, huh? That fits." Jo thought of her vision of a big room with rows of narrow beds. "And guess what? The guy who writes in my journal — he mentioned 'the Sisters.' With a capital S."

"What makes you so sure he was a guy?" Mel asked.

"Don't know. I don't have a name for him. It just feels like he's a he."

"Here we are," Calvin announced. He turned the station wagon into a side street, circled a grey stone building with white pillars framing the entrance, and found the parking lot. "Burfast Public Library. Unless you know all you need to now?"

"I don't think so. I want pictures. Newspaper articles. Archives!"

Mel sighed heavily.

They found the reference department and a friendly librarian, but the answer to Jo's question was disappointing. "The Spin River Orphanage?" she said. "Sorry, we have nothing. And I've had this question before, so I know the county museum has nothing either. You'd do better to ask the sisters themselves."

"You mean, they're still around?"

"Yes, although they aren't running orphanages these days. They're a teaching order. Their house is on Huron Street in Toronto, south of the university."

"Yes!" Mel exulted.

"Would they have anything about the old orphanage?" Jo asked.

"It's your best bet. They keep their archives there and they're quite ferocious about not letting anything go." She grinned.

"But would they let us in?"

"Ask for Sister Jerome Timmins. You'll see. Here's the address."

Chapter 16

AN HOUR AND a half later Calvin parked the station wagon by the curb in front of a big, untidy, old-fashioned brick house. They crawled stiffly out of the car and stood in a row on the sidewalk, staring.

"This can't be it," Jo said. She wasn't sure what she'd been expecting — a high wall and a closed gate with a peephole, maybe — but not this. Despite its fancy brickwork and extra gables and turrets and bits of stained glass here and there, the house looked... well, normal. More than anything, it looked comfortable. It fit right in with the other big old houses on this tree-lined street.

"This is a convent?" Mel whispered.

Calvin pointed at a bronze plaque bolted into the brickwork beside the front door. ST. INNOCENT HOUSE, it said. "Seems so."

Mel poked him in the ribs. "You can't go in. No boys allowed!"

"We'll see." After looking around for a bell and not finding one, he pushed the door open. Inside they found a hallway smelling of old wood, furniture wax, and fresh coffee. An open door on the right was labelled OFFICE. VISITORS PLEASE CHECK IN. Inside they found a reception desk with an elderly black woman sitting behind it. Jo wondered if she was a nun, then decided not. She wasn't wearing a habit.

She smiled at them. "What can I do for you?"

"We're, um, looking for Sister Jerome Timmins."

The woman looked doubtful. "She's very busy."

"Um..." Then Jo remembered. "We want to show her this." She

dug the silver medal out of her pocket and held it out, turning it to show back and front.

She peered at it, then sat back. "Well, isn't that interesting! She'll certainly want to see that." She gave them an encouraging nod and pointed at the door. "Along the hall, up the stairs, turn right."

"RANSOM." Sister Jerome couldn't stop smiling. "Really! This is so cool!"

The St. Innocent archivist wasn't anything like what Jo had been expecting, either. To start with, she was about forty years younger than the original picture in Jo's mind. A framed master's degree in history hanging on the wall was only a year old. She wore jeans, a red cotton shirt, and sandals. Her short, dark hair fluffed up as if she'd been rubbing her head in furious thought.

"I'm writing a book, a history of the order," she told them, almost as soon as they were in the door. "My predecessor left me all this." She waved a hand at the cartons stacked along the walls and the crammed bookshelves. "Not one word of it digitized! Just getting things on disc will take me half a lifetime!" Her eyes shone with glee.

When Calvin's name came up, Sister Jerome pounced on it. "Ransom! Any relation to Jeremy Ransom?"

"My great-grandfather." He showed her the medal.

"That's *awesome!*" She burrowed into a cupboard in the corner of the room and backed out holding a digital camera. "May I?" At Calvin's nod she photographed the medal, back and front, then took a picture of Calvin holding it. She handed the medal back reluctantly. "Don't suppose you'd be willing to part with this, eh?"

"Well, it's not really mine. It's kind of a family treasure. Since it's the only thing of my great-granddad's we have from his early days, you see."

"And did he ever talk about those early days?" Sister Jerome set down the camera and picked up a voice recorder.

"Never, my dad says. Sorry. I don't know anything about it, he died long before I was born."

"Oh, well." Sister Jerome looked disappointed. Then she grinned. "Never mind, it's a kick to meet an actual descendant of the notorious Jeremy."

"Notorious? Why?"

"Come out into the back yard. I'll tell you all about it."

They sat in Muskoka chairs in the shade of a chestnut tree drinking orange juice, while Sister Jerome enthusiastically recounted the history of the Sisters of St. Innocent. From its beginning, the order was dedicated to caring for and educating orphaned children. The Spin River building was only one of several orphanages run by the order, but it was considered the top of the line.

"In fact, it was a model institution for the time. The children got plenty of outdoor exercise and nourishing food and proper health care. And they were schooled too, they got an education so they could go out in the world and make their living. Some went into trades or shops or farming, a few went to teacher's college or university. It was a *good* place." She thumped the broad arm of her chair. "That's why people were so shocked when the house burned down in 1924, and they found it was arson!"

"Arson! So, who did it?" Mel asked. "And why?"

"Who? They're pretty sure it was Calvin's great-granddad, Jeremy." Sister Jerome gave Calvin a playful punch on the arm.

Calvin said nothing. He swirled the juice in his bottle and looked as if he was working out a puzzle in his head.

"Why do they think it was him?" Jo asked.

"It was deliberately started, that was proven. But whoever did it made sure nobody would get hurt. The staff and children were on an outing to the harvest fair in Burfast — all except two of the kitchen workers, and Jeremy. He'd stayed behind with a cold."

"So maybe it was one of the..." Mel began.

Sister Jerome was already shaking her head. "They went to the village to get supplies. All this is from the Reverend Mother's account, and she was a dragon for details, that one! Jeremy was the only person not accounted for."

"Did he admit setting the fire?" Jo asked.

"No, but he never denied it, either."

"What happened to him then? Did the sisters toss him in jail?"

Sister Jerome laughed. "No, they didn't do anything. I'm not sure why. They weren't softies, you know." She looked at Calvin. "I was hoping you'd have more information about why he did it — if he ever talked about it in the family."

"No, he never did, according to my dad. He, my dad, said he learned to stop asking."

"Then what about your great-grandmother, did she drop any hints? Jeremy married another of the kids from the orphanage, but I guess you know that."

"Yeah. Sorry, nothing there either. But..." Calvin took a slow swig of juice. "Maybe you should look at what came after, what the result was. Maybe that would be a clue."

"The children were sent away, of course. They were dispersed to other orphanages, or adopted by local families. Some older ones, like Jeremy, were placed as apprentices. He would have been sixteen at that time."

"So they never came back to that place," Jo said. She caught Calvin's eye. He nodded.

"Right." Sister Jerome intercepted the glance. "There was some talk of rebuilding, but the sisters thought the site itself might have been unwholesome. So they decided against it."

"Un-unwholesome?" Mel asked nervously.

"There was rather a high rate of illness and death at the orphanage, despite all the good nursing." Sister Jerome tapped the arm of her chair, still looking thoughtful. "Higher than the norm even then, and this was in the bad old days before penicillin. You should take a look in the cemetery at MacPhee. They're all there, all the little grave markers. It's very sad to see."

They sat in silence for a few moments while they finished their juice. Then Jo said, "We walked by the cemetery yesterday. I found a gravestone outside the fence. Not inside, though I'm pretty sure there was room. Why would that be?"

"Outside? That usually means the person took their own life and couldn't be buried in consecrated ground."

Mel sat up. "But that's awful!"

"I know, but that's how they did things, back then. Not any more, of course. Did you find a name?" she asked Jo.

"Ellen Quinn." Jo thought a moment. "Dates, I think... 1875-1897. She was only twenty-two."

"So young. That is sad." Sister Jerome stared into space. "Ellen Quinn... Quinn... Rings a bell... No, can't recall. I'll see what I can find out." She pulled a notebook from her jeans pocket and wrote down the information, as well as Frieda's land line phone number.

"Um, about all that illness." Jo avoided Calvin's eye: Sister Jerome was too sharp. "Did they ever figure out why?"

"Damp night air," Sister Jerome said crisply. "Folks in those days had a horror of it." She suddenly smiled and jumped from her chair. "Want to see some pictures?"

They went back inside and she brought out brown-toned photographs in acid-free folders. Picture after picture of solemn children in dark clothing, lined up in rows, backed by nuns in spotless white habits, on the lawn in front of a three-storey brick building. Calvin bent over one of them, then stood back. "Who's that?" His forefinger hovered over one child who stood at the end of the row.

Sister Jerome picked up the photo and checked it front and back. Jo looked over her shoulder. The boy Calvin had pointed out — small, round-faced, about six or seven, with a head of soft dark curls — was noticeably handsomer than the others, but otherwise there was no reason to single him out.

"No names, just a year. 1896. Why?" Sister Jerome cocked her head at Calvin. "It wouldn't be Jeremy, he wasn't even born then."

"No, no, I..." Calvin kept backing away. "I just thought he looked like..." He shot a *help me* look at Jo. She jumped in with a question she'd been wanting to ask.

"Do you have any photos of the inside of the building?"

"Tons!" Sister Jerome spread them on the table. Photos of high-ceilinged rooms, dark wooden floors gleaming with polish, large windows with billowing white curtains.

And dormitories with rows of narrow white-blanketed beds, each with its little cupboard and small oval braided mat. Jo's heart thumped. And a corridor with … with … Yes, there they were.

"Are those gas lights?" Calvin asked.

"No, electric. Made to look like gas — that was the style then. They were newly installed when that picture was taken. Pretty, aren't they?" Sister Jerome handed him a large magnifying glass. He offered it to Jo, but she shook her head.

"Are they etched with morning glories?"

Calvin aimed the glass at the photo, then lowered it and looked at her. "Uh-huh."

"How did you know that?" Sister Jerome gave Jo a piercing stare.

"I... um... guessed," Jo said lamely.

They left a few minutes later. "Here's my card," Sister Jerome said to Calvin, at the door. "Feel free to get in touch. Any of you." Her eyes moved, not smiling now, over all their faces.

"That's so weird," Mel said, as they walked back to the car.

"What?" Jo slouched along, hands in pockets, thinking of the morning glories.

"Like, why does she have a man's name?"

"It's her religious name," Calvin said. "She's named after St. Jerome. Which I guess makes sense."

"Why?" Jo stopped with a hand on the passenger door handle.

"Jerome is a doctor of the Church. Doctor means a man of learning," he said to Mel, who had taken breath to speak. "He's also the patron saint of librarians."

"Very cool," Jo said. "And you know all this how?"

He shrugged. "I'm Catholic."

"Ah." *So much I don't know about you!*

"She helped a lot, didn't she?" Mel said.

"Yeah. She's nice and I like her." Jo glanced back at the house. "I don't feel good about keeping things from her. She knew we were holding back, too."

"It wouldn't have done any good to tell her." Calvin climbed back into the Ford. "She wouldn't have believed."

"I'm not so sure. Okay, it's open-up time." Jo turned to face him in the front seat. "What was all that about the boy in the photo?"

Calvin paused with his hand on the ignition. He opened and closed his mouth, then sighed. "I've dreamed him. For years. Nearly knocked me over, seeing that face in the picture."

"He must be one of the ones who... died," Mel said in a small voice. "Back then."

"Guess so." Calvin started the engine. "But he wasn't the only one. So, why him?"

"And why you?" Jo asked. "What's your connection to him? He died before Jeremy was born, so that can't be it."

Calvin shook his head and drove.

Chapter 17

"AND NOW," Mel sang, "now for some serious shopping. Boys and girls, we're goin' downtown!"

Jo was happy to take her cue from Mel and say nothing more about what they'd learned that morning. Even Calvin, who by the look of him didn't shop much, went along with the fiction that they had nothing on their minds except buying stuff. They parked again, agonizing about the sky-high fees; browsed the music stores, the shoe stores, the fashion stores. Mel and Jo collected several bulging plastic shopping bags each. Calvin bought nothing, but he didn't seem to mind being dragged into every second store. He even agreed to carry most of the bags.

They bought lunch from a samosa cart on the street and sat on an iron bench to eat while a river of cars and people poured past. After buying the printer cartridge for Frieda they walked to the boutique district, where they ogled costly outfits in tiny shop windows.

They hardly stopped laughing. The air sparkled, and it wasn't only the sunshine. Spinbrook House and its secrets could have been a thousand miles away, or a story from someone else's troubled life.

And then, with a jolt, reality thudded back into place. Jo glanced in passing into the window of a small commercial art gallery, and stopped dead. "Omigod, look!" She pointed. Mel, behind her, gasped.

"Hey, is that — "

"Yes! It is, I'm sure of it!"

"Get any closer, you'll leave nose prints," Calvin said drily. They ignored him.

"It's so beautiful!" Mel breathed. "And so real!"

"Too real," Jo said.

Whoever had painted this stretch of the Spin River had been standing on the shore near the stepping stones, on the side across from the house. The waterfall and the dark pool below it were so true to reality that for a moment Jo smelled wet rock and pine resin. The back of her neck went cold.

"It's not just that it's so real," she murmured, staring. "There's something... about..." That pool. It seemed to radiate darkness. And when she looked hard, that small shape curled around a rock at the pool's edge looked less like a leaf and more like a hand.

"Somebody else knows." She looked from Mel's frightened face to Calvin's guarded one. Finding no help there, she bent close to the glass to read the signature scrawled in the lower right corner of the painting. Impossible to make it out. She straightened up. "Come on, we've got to find out who this is!"

"Um... Jo..." Calvin said, but she was already pushing the door open. The gallery was long and narrow, with soft lighting and pale grey carpeting. It smelled like fresh paint. A bearded man looked up from a table at the back of the room, fingers poised over a laptop keyboard.

"Excuse me! That painting in the window — the one with the pool. Who did it?"

The man frowned at Jo over little half-glasses and looked as if he was going to tell her to go away and stop making such a noise. Then he looked past her and beamed. "Calvin! *Comment ça va?*" He got up and came forward, both hands outstretched.

"Oh, uh, Gilles. Fine, thanks. Um, these are my friends. Jo. Melanie. Just stopped in to say hi. We're going now, so long." He was herding them back toward the door as he spoke.

"Wait a minute!" Jo dodged his arm. She looked from him to Gilles. "How do you know Calvin?"

"He is one of my artists — my youngest, in fact. He painted that landscape in the window."

"Calvin?" She gaped at the man and pointed back over her shoulder. "Painted that?"

"Among others, yes." Gilles looked amused. "He has a well-developed talent for one so young. You didn't know this about your friend?"

Jo's cheeks were still burning when they stepped out into the street again. "I feel like the world's biggest fool!"

"It's all your fault, Calvin." Mel wagged a finger at him. "For making such a mystery of it. Well, now we know what you keep locked in your room."

"No you don't," he said coolly. He walked a little apart from them, hands full of shopping bags, eyes scanning the passing crowd.

"Let me guess." Jo took a longer stride to keep up with him. "You keep your painting secret because your parents are against it. They're hard-headed folks and they don't want their son to end up a starving artist in a garret and if they knew what you were doing, they'd be really upset. Am I right?"

He grinned. "Way off. My parents are great about it. Well, they were kind of doubtful for a while. But my first gallery sale reassured my dad. And my mom thinks I'm destined to be the next Andrew Wyeth."

"Then why?"

He walked in silence for a moment. "The landscapes, even the ones of the river, aren't the problem," he said at last. "It's the other paintings. I call them my nightmare pictures. I don't let people see them. They bother people. Especially my mom."

"Nightmare pictures," Mel said, too brightly. "What a surprise! Well, we eat nightmares for breakfast, don't we, Jo? We'd love to see them!"

"Don't be too sure," Calvin said.

IT WAS LATE afternoon by the time they turned off the county road into the gravel driveway of Spinbrook House. Another car was parked near the front door and a youngish, balding man stood beside it talking to Mrs. Rhodes. He climbed into his car and drove away as Mel and Jo unloaded their shopping bags from the station wagon.

"There you are!" The nurse smiled at them as they walked up. "I'm glad you're back. It's time for me to leave, and Mrs. Stone is still tied up in her work. That was Dr. Bliss," she added.

"Oh, good! Has he..." Jo looked past her and spotted Lewis in his wheelchair, sitting in the dappled sunlight under the pergola. She lowered her voice. "He didn't call an ambulance?"

"No. It's too soon to tell if Lew should be back in hospital, he says. He's taken blood samples and he'll have tests done."

"Lew's had dozens of tests," Mel said sourly. "They never show anything wrong."

"Doctor says he needs more fresh air and sunshine, and perhaps a course of vitamin B12. Lew may be anemic. But there's nothing seriously wrong, he says."

He says, Jo noted. "And what do you think?"

"Well, I..." Mrs. Rhodes looked back at Lew and waved cheerfully. He didn't move. She let her gaze move over the house, then looked from Mel to Jo. "The doc's not a local man. He doesn't know the stories."

"About the orphanage, you mean?"

"That, yes. But newer stories, too. One of the families that lived in this house before Mr. and Mrs. Stone, they had three young children. Back in the 'eighties, that was. The two youngest... they just wasted away."

"From what?" Mel demanded. "I mean, there had to be some medical reason. Right?"

"So you'd think. But I never heard of any." She picked up her bag and turned toward her car, then turned back. "And they weren't the only ones. Between us three, and I know this sounds irrational, I wouldn't let a child of mine stay here, not for a single day." She looked over at Lew again. "You keep an eye on him!"

"We will," Jo said. "We will."

Chapter 18

THEY ARE DOWN on the grass in front of the house, Jo wrote in her journal after dinner. *Mel dug up some old croquet equipment from somewhere and got Calvin to help her set it up, and now they are hitting balls around the lawn. I think it diverts Lew, a little. It's hard to tell what he thinks. He hardly reacts, any more. He never smiles. It's like almost all the life has gone out of him in the last couple of days.*

She glanced at the opposite page, but the invisible writer was keeping his head down. She had covered several pages describing the events of the day, giving him plenty of time to join in, but so far, nothing. It was still a mystery why he came, never mind how.

She hoped he would come back. Strangely, she was looking forward to seeing him again — if you could call it seeing, when not even a hand appeared. She felt they had problems in common. And she liked the tone of what he wrote. He cared about the people he was living with.

I worry about Mel too, she wrote. *She hates being inside the house, especially at night. And that's funny, because it seems to me the — whatever it is — belongs outside, in the dark places of the stream. This threat, enemy, curse — I don't even know what to call it. If only we could understand what it is!*

One thing really jumped out at me today, looking at those old photos with Sister Jerome. All those nuns in their white clothes. So much like that — whatever it was — that I saw in the corridor last night. And now I'm certain that corridor was in the old orphanage. Maybe it was in the same physical space, ninety years ago, as this third-floor gallery is now. So, what am I seeing? Am I simply reliving something that happened long ago but in the same spot? But if that's so, then how is Lew involved? What's happening to him? And why —

She glanced at the opposite page and stopped writing. Then laid down her pen, sat quietly and watched.

...beginning to think that someone is helping it get in. Its proper place is not here, in a human house. It needs to be invited in, I think. Would one of the Sisters be doing it? Not on purpose, I'm sure of that. But what might happen in dreams? Night is when it is strongest.

Poor little Esther — they moved her into the infirmary, but she died this morning. Marie says we must do something soon, and I agree. But...

The writing faded. "Poor little Esther," Jo muttered. "Poor Lew."

She wrote down the message word for word, as far as she could remember. Then she went downstairs and out the front door. Mel was nowhere to be seen, and Frieda had taken Lew inside. Calvin was pulling the croquet hoops out of the grass and collecting the balls and mallets. Jo helped him stow them away in the shed behind the garage.

"I wish," she said, giving the last mallet an angry swish through the air before hanging it in its rack, "I wish we could give this whatever-it-is a good wallop and scare it away for good!"

"Nice if it were that easy." Calvin closed the shed door.

"We've got to do something. Soon!" Standing beside the garage in the yellow sunset light, she told him what Mrs. Rhodes had said. "That doctor," she added, "makes me think of those people at the orphanage, all those years ago. Anemia! Damp night air! How blind can you be?"

"They can't help it. Something in their minds keeps them from seeing the worst."

"But Lew sees it. And the guy who writes in my journal, he saw it. And you and I…" She looked at the trees overhanging the stream. The shadows were already thickening under the canopy. "We can see it. We know it's there. Why us?"

"Isn't it obvious?" His blue eyes darkened. "In Lew's case, anyway."

"You mean…" She went cold.

"It takes the young ones. Always. Like in the orphanage. The littlest ones are best — it can take them easiest."

Dread and horror made her sharp. "And us, where do we fit in? We're not so little any more."

"I was, once." His lips barely moved. He watched her eyes.

It took her a few moments to work it out. "You mean, you…" She glanced towards where the stream sang invisibly down the hill behind the trees. "But you didn't…"

"Yeah, me. And no, I didn't die. Or not for long."

"When…" She seemed to lack enough breath to finish her sentences.

"I was seven." He poked a finger at her. "But you're the mystery, Josephine Meurig. You're a stranger to this place, right? So what makes you such easy meat for this thing?"

"I… I don't know." She looked away. "I don't understand."

"You psychic, maybe?" His tone was mild, but his eyes were boring holes in her. "You see ghosts and ghoulies?"

"No! Never! And now you're trying to rattle me."

"Well, I'm rattled." He lifted his wrist, where the white mark still showed. "I'll tell you my story if you'll tell me yours."

"Exchange secrets?" she said warily. It hadn't worked all that well with Mel.

"Sure. C'mon, I'll show you."

He led the way at a brisk walk around the house and down

through the trees to the stepping stones. He went over them almost at a run. Jo followed close on his heels. She carefully did not look into the dark pool. "Where — are we — going?" she gasped.

"Not far." He walked along the south shore of the stream, down river, until they came to a cleared space under the trees. A blackened circle of rocks near the water's edge showed where somebody had lit a fire, not long ago.

"Good campsite, this." Calvin looked around. "Big enough for a good-sized tent. My parents like to camp, especially my dad. He loves fishing."

"Hm." Jo looked upstream toward the waterfall. "This isn't where you painted that picture."

"No, I painted that from here." He tapped his forehead. "I never come to this place. I try to stay away from the stream altogether. Don't care for it." He jammed his hands in his pockets.

"And that's because…"

"When I was seven, my parents and I camped here overnight. Just us three. Nell — she's my kid sister — she wasn't born yet. I must've wandered away in the night, because when they woke up and found me missing and went looking, they found me in that pool up there."

"That pool," Jo breathed.

"I was at the edge, half in, half out. The half that was in was the top end. I was drowned."

"You mean, really…"

"Dead. Right. Heart stopped and all. But they got it going again, so I couldn't have been dead for long." He shook his head. "You understand, I don't remember any of this. I only found out later, from my parents, and they never liked to talk about it. My mom will, a bit, but my dad just says he aged ten years that day. They blamed themselves for not watching me better."

After a silence made up of water sounds and birdsong, Jo touched his arm. "But you survived. You must've been one tough little guy."

He gave her a small smile. "Dunno. Ever since, I've had these nightmares. I think they're the shut-away part of my mind, trying to tell me what really happened."

"And that's what you paint? Those paintings that you keep secret? You paint your nightmares."

"Right. You can see why I don't let many people see them."

The sun was almost down. Time enough to deliver on her half of the bargain, before this spot became uncomfortably dark. "The reason I came to Spinbrook House — I was diagnosed with PTSD. Post-traumatic stress disorder. Sounds to me as if you've got the same thing, or something close to it." She sat down on the grass, which still held a hint of the day's warmth.

Calvin settled beside her. They both watched the house on the hill, no lights on, dark and glassy against the glowing sky. "I have a simpler explanation," he said. "I'm being haunted."

"Is that a metaphor?"

"No."

Ghosts. She wrapped her hands around her crossed ankles, covering the white mark. "O-*kay*. Well, I'm haunted too, by... well, memories. That I can't shake. It all goes back to this stupid phobia of mine. I've had it for as long as I can remember. Fear of dark water. You know, water you can't see into."

"I'd call that a reasonable fear, not a phobia. Swimming in dark water is risky."

"Yes, but with me it's not sensible caution, it's..." She gripped her ankles tighter. "Terror. The kind that makes you sweat and throw up and your heart beat so hard you think you're going to die."

"Okay, phobia." He sounded tranquil. He watched the house. She was grateful he kept his eyes off her while she spilled this pain and shame.

"So my big brother Evan, two years older than me, last summer he told me he was going to cure me." In spite of herself she smiled. "He said he had this phobia himself, and it never really goes away, but you can learn to control it. And the way to do that..." She took a breath. "He had this thing he repeated. 'You have to go through the darkness to reach the light. It's the only way.' He had a plan."

As they sat there on the cooling grass and watched the sunset slowly fade from the sky, she told Calvin about that day last summer.

Chapter 19

THEY WERE TAKING a week's vacation at an oceanside inn on Nova Scotia's South Shore: the whole family, Evan and Jo and their parents. Evan had been there before and he knew the good diving spots along the coast. He was an experienced scuba diver, and he'd also done free diving — going down without breathing gear. There was a network of caves near the inn, some of the caves linked by underwater tunnels.

"So there was this cave, not high but deep, and way in the back, where the light from the cave mouth just barely reached, there was a wide pool, black as tar. We had no lights with us, though we had wetsuits — because, you know, the waters off Nova Scotia are numbing even in July — and I had a waterproof chronograph watch so I could time Evan. See, he had this three-part plan. He was always such an organizer!" She tried to laugh.

"The first time, he would go in alone. There was a tunnel that opened at the back of the pool, opposite from where we stood, a couple of yards below the surface, and he would swim down there and go through — the tunnel was only wide enough for one person, and not all that long, you could get through it in roughly five seconds, he said. You just had to be careful not to bump your head on the ceiling, where some rocks stuck down. And when you got in the tunnel you would start to see a bit of light, and then it would bend and there would be lots of light, and then you were through into the pool in the next cave. And that cave was half open to the sky and the pool in it was as clear as your bath. And up you'd go to the surface to fill your lungs.

"So the plan was, he would go through alone the first time. I would time him with the watch, and he promised the round trip should take no more than thirty seconds. Maybe a bit more, depending on how long he spent in the far pool, loading up with oxygen. After that, we would go through together, with Evan in the lead. And the third time, I would go through by myself. 'Remember! Through darkness to the light,' he said. 'The only way.' And he gave me a hug and laughed and said 'I'll be back!' And he dove in. And the water splashed and he was gone."

And that was the last time I saw my brother alive.

She didn't think she'd said that aloud, but Calvin, still cross-legged, turned his whole body toward her. "If this is too hard, let it go," he said. "This exchange was a stupid idea."

She was tempted. He's kind, she thought. So kind. And such a good listener.

So I owe him the truth.

"I'm okay." She cleared her throat and got a better grip on her ankles. Then went on to tell how she'd stood at the edge of that inky pool, watching the second hand creep around the glowing dial of the stopwatch. Ten, twelve, fifteen... twenty, twenty-five... thirty... forty...

"I should have gone in then. I shouldn't have waited. I told myself he was treading water in the far pool, catching his breath. I thought he must have lost track of how long he was taking. But any second now, any second... I stopped looking at the watch. I looked at the pool. No hands came poking up, no head shaking off water — "

"Jo. Let go."

He'd pried her hands from around her ankles and shut her fists inside the cage of his own long fingers. There were small bloody marks on both her ankles.

"Come on, Jo. You can stop now."

"No. No, I can't. I suddenly felt this terrible panic and I dove in, not thinking of the dark, only Evan, where's Evan? I found the back wall of the pool and felt down and there was the opening, and there was a little light coming in, but not much, because there was— there was something stuck in there, a couple of feet in. I pushed at it and it was a — a face. A head. It was Evan. He wasn't moving. I mean he, he was moving, but not by himself. I think the water was moving him because his hands were drifting around like... like..."

"Easy. Easy."

Jo swallowed bile. She breathed, in, out. Reached for words. "I couldn't understand why he was stuck. But I felt along and he was caught — his zipper pull, you know that cord that hangs from a wet-suit zipper in back, you pull on it to zip the suit up to the neck — it was caught in a crack in the rocks and I thought that was holding him, but when I pulled on it, it pulled free. And then I starting pulling on him, but I... ran out of air..." She stopped, breathed. "I had to..."

I left him to drown.

Calvin's hands held on.

"I, I had to go up for air. Up and down. I think maybe four times. I pulled him out, finally, and up we went together and I pulled him to shore and then... I knew before, but I hoped... Now I saw. He was dead. He was dead."

She pulled her hands free and covered her face. Calvin's arms went around her, gentle, warm. He held her and they rocked back and forth together. For a long time she let herself be cradled, safe and warm, no need to remember or think. Then she straightened up and dropped her hands. When Calvin's arms slipped away, she almost asked for them back, but knew it wouldn't help get her head straight.

She scrubbed her face with her hands and cleared her throat. "There isn't a lot left to tell. It turns out he was dead long before I went down after him. Seems he hit his head on that tunnel roof, hard enough to knock him out or stun him, and then he... drowned. I couldn't have saved him — they kept telling me — unless I'd been right there when it happened."

"I kinda figured," Calvin said. "But that wasn't the end, was it?"

"No. The dreams started right away and they never really stopped. And the fear. One glimpse of dark water — even on television, for heaven's sake! — started me shaking. I slept badly. I wasn't much good at work, what with the fatigue and trouble concentrating. And I started to doubt myself. I used to be fairly confident, there wasn't much I wouldn't try, at least once." She laughed, a better effort this time. "But no more. I felt like a piece of crap, to tell the truth. I let my brother drown."

"But you didn't," Calvin said gently.

"Yeah, my head said that, but the rest of me... well, one time I thought I might as well go back there to that pool where Evan died and go down and stay down."

She looked at him, at what she could see of his face in the thickening dark. He was watching her intently, his eyes not asking anything, not accusing, not protesting. He just waited.

"You know, most people don't get it." She shook her head, remembering. "I learned to keep what I felt to myself. Except for a few special people. Like my mom and dad, they understood. But this guy I knew — Graeme — he didn't get it at all."

"Old boyfriend?"

Her eyebrows flew up. "Yeah, since high school. How'd you guess?"

"Tone of voice. Regret, anger."

"Yes, that sums it up. He said I used to be so strong, so solid. He said I wasn't the girl he thought he knew. Said I was taking the easy way out. So that was it for Graeme. Poof, gone."

"You don't still want to go jump in the lake, I hope."

"No, Dr. Klein talked me through that. It was when I started having those thoughts that I knew I needed help and I went to her. She helped a lot. She said, don't remember Evan by what happened to him that day. That's not even a tiny fraction of what he was. Remember him by what he said to you. Through darkness to the light, it's the only way."

"Your brother sounds to me like a good guy."

"He was." She took a long breath, let it out, and felt a heaviness lift. *And so are you.* "I'm on a journey now," she added, "and coming here to Spinbrook House was supposed to help me along the road."

"Mistake, maybe. You won't get better sticking around here." He stood up and held out a hand to help her up. She didn't need it, but took it anyway. She liked the way his hands felt, lean and strong.

LIGHT CAUGHT Jo's eyes. Upstream, above the waterfall, Spinbrook House was lighting up. The Cataract Room was a glowing bubble on the side of the hill. A slim, dark figure watched them from behind the greenish glass. "There's Mel." Jo waved and the small figure waved back.

"There's the real mystery, right there," she added. "Mel. Something about this house terrifies her. But it isn't the pool, it's something inside the house. Do you think — is it possible she sees that white figure, like Lew does? That it comes to her room and... No, that can't be it."

"No, because Mel's not dying or anywhere close to it."

"But something's wrong with her, and she won't open up." Jo

watched Mel turn and go inside the living room. "She won't talk about what she's really afraid of."

"Maybe there's something she thinks you won't like to hear."

"What could that be?"

"Dunno. I only wonder."

"You do know. What is it?"

He shook his head. The quiet, closed look on his face told her she'd be wasting her breath.

"Okay, Calvin. At least I know your dreadful secret, now. Are you going to let me see those paintings?"

"Not now. Not at night. Tomorrow, in daylight. Maybe." He started back along the path bordering the stream. Over his shoulder he said, "You should think about leaving."

"We've been through all that. I'm not running out!"

"But what could you actually do here? Realistically."

They crossed the stepping stones. Jo kept her eyes on the stones and Calvin's back. She caught up with him on the far shore and stopped him with a hand on his arm. "I have an idea," she said.

Chapter 20

"MRS. RHODES SAID to keep an eye on Lew," Jo went on, as they climbed the path to the house. "I think that's a good idea. Especially at night. Let's find Mel."

Mel was on the terrace outside her bedroom, sitting on the stone floor against the wall of the house, staring at nothing. She was wearing those big earphones and nursing the vintage CD player in her lap. Jo had to shake her arm twice before Mel slipped the earphones off her head.

"Here's the plan." Jo sat down beside her. "It's really simple — it's just to keep Lew safe until we can think of something permanent."

"Okay, well?"

"We'll take turns watching him at night. We'll never leave him alone."

"What, stay up half the night?" Mel looked astonished.

"A third of the night, only." Calvin folded his long legs and settled beside Jo. "I'll be taking a shift too."

"This is silly. Watching him won't help."

"Of course it will." Jo frowned. "What's the matter with you?"

"He's sick. You can't stop that. You can't cure him." Mel slipped the earphones back onto her head. Jo lifted them off again.

"He's not sick. Something's getting at him. Haven't you seen or heard anything?"

"No!" Mel shook her head until her hair flew.

"You must have. I have, and I've only been here a few days.

You've been here weeks!"

"Well, I'm not the one with PTSD, am I?"

Jo stood up, not trusting herself to reply.

"No bad dreams?" Calvin inquired blandly.

"Me? No! I sleep like a log. I never hear anything." Mel pushed the earphones back into place and closed her eyes.

"Sleep like a log? Never leave your room?"

"You left your room last night," Jo pointed out. "You must've heard some — "

"I told you, no!" Mel's eyes snapped open and she gave Jo a strange look. Fear or hatred, Jo didn't know which. She jumped up, pushed past them, and went into her bedroom. The door slammed, the lock clicked.

Jo stared at the locked door. "What's got into her?"

"Good way to put it."

"And that means?"

"Dunno." He stood up. "At least, I'm not sure. I could be way wrong."

"More secrets?" She yawned and stretched. Last night's few hours of sleep hadn't been nearly enough. "Well, she's no help to us tonight. That leaves you and me, Calvin. If you really meant what you said."

"I always mean what I say."

"Funny thing, I believe you."

"I'll take the first watch."

"No, I'll go first. That way I can explain to Lew what we're doing. You get some sleep, until… when?"

"Two a.m., let's say. Think you can stay awake till then?"

"Piece of cake."

IT WAS A LITTLE past 10 o'clock when Jo slipped out of her room into the gallery. She nearly fell over a sleeping bag. Calvin's flaxen mop poked out of it at the open end. He snored gently.

Jo stood smiling down at him. It's true, she thought. People look so endearingly harmless when they're asleep. Harmless or not, she felt safer knowing he was within call.

She stepped past him, walked softly along the gallery to Lew's room and opened the door. Only the pink-glowing nightlight was on. Lew was a small hump under the white coverlet. The shine of his eyes showed that he was awake.

"Only me," Jo said. "We're going to keep you company tonight. First me, then Calvin. Is that okay with you?"

His chin moved down a centimeter. *Yes.*

"You don't look a bit sleepy. Want a story?" She held up a book she'd found on the shelves in the living room. "It's *The Secret Garden*." Lew made a tiny nod.

"Thought you might. Here, I'll snuggle in next to you. Good thing I brought a flashlight, huh? Okay, here we go. Chapter One, 'There Is No One Left'."

Lew didn't drop off to sleep, the way he'd done the last time Jo read to him. But after about fifteen minutes, something in his face told her that he was miles away from whatever he feared. The story had worked its magic.

When the door opened, the spell broke and his face tightened up all over. Jo's heart thumped. Then she laughed softly. "It's only Calvin. Why aren't you asleep, Calvin?"

"I was asleep. Had a dream." He nodded at her. "Yeah, that kind of dream. Come out here a sec. Something out here you should see."

"But..." She glanced at Lew and back at Calvin. *I can't leave him.*

"Only for a minute. It's important."

"Oh, all right. Lew? I'll be back in a jiff, okay?"

He shaped *No* with his mouth. Jo felt torn in half.

"Look — " She held his hand. "You'll be fine. You'll be safe. And I'll be right back, I promise. Okay?" She watched for the tiny nod, and gave his hand a squeeze.

"This better be important," she muttered to Calvin as the door shut behind her.

"It is, but we're nearly too late. Hurry, and be quiet!"

He grabbed her hand and pulled her over to the balustrade. A dark figure was walking silently down the stairs, eclipsing the tiny foot-lights in passing. As it turned on the landing and started down the next flight, the dim light showed it was Mel. Her face was white and smooth, like a mask. She was wearing shorts and a T-shirt, and her feet were bare.

Jo looked at Calvin. "So?" she whispered.

"I've seen this before, once or twice this summer, from outside the house. I've never seen exactly what happens."

"What is she doing, sleepwalking? Maybe we'd better wake Frieda."

"No time." He started down the stairs without looking to see if she was following. Jo glanced along the gallery to Lew's closed door, then made up her mind. *I'll quick see what's going on. Then I'll dash back upstairs.*

She caught up to Calvin on the ground floor. He was watching Mel disappear, step by step, down the stairwell that led to the cellar. The only light came from the baseboard guide lights. Mel moved without a sound. The voice of the waterfall, outside the Cataract Room, was suddenly loud.

"What is she doing?" Jo whispered. "She hates the cellar. Why is she going down there?"

"Wish I knew," Calvin muttered back. "Wait and see."

They waited at the top of the well. Nothing at all was visible below, not even the cellar door. "She doesn't have a flashlight," Jo said suddenly. "She's gone down into the pitch-dark cellar at night, without a flashlight. This is all wrong!"

She started down the stairs, but Calvin slipped past her and barred the way. "Not yet!"

"Something bad is happening, I know it!"

"Which is exactly why we're staying here!"

Jo decided not to argue. Just as she was planning where to aim the first kick, a white glow appeared below them. It radiated through the cracks around the door. Only a moment, and then it faded, leaving sickly green after-images.

Jo blinked. "Mel?" No answer. She shoved with all her might at Calvin's arm.

"Not yet!" he snapped.

"But she could be hurt!"

"And it may not be something you can face. Just once, Jo, don't rush in where — "

"Wait — she's coming up." Jo let go of his arm.

The door squeaked faintly as it opened. Calvin and Jo retreated to the top the stairs. As silent as before, Mel climbed up into the light. If she saw the two standing above her, she gave no sign. She walked past them as if they were invisible and started up the open spiral that led to the upper floors. A breath of cool air came with her, and the scent of wet earth and stone.

"Still sleepwalking?" Jo whispered.

"I… guess…" Calvin frowned as he followed Mel with his eyes. "Something's wrong."

"If you mean something's wrong with Mel, yeah, anybody can see that. But right now I've got to get back to Lew." Her voice sharpened. "What's this?"

Something else was coming up the stairs. Its steps dragged. It made a low sobbing sound. Jo dug her fingers into Calvin's arm. When it was near enough she could hear what it was saying.

"Oh, help... Help me... "

"Mel?" Jo stepped forward.

"Jo? What are you... Where..." Mel clutched at her hair. "What's happening to me?"

Jo thought, *Lew.* Next moment she was flying up the stairs. Feet pounded behind her. On the second floor landing the staircase changed, its smooth whiteness darkening, the steel handrail becoming wood. Cold, wet wood. Jo snatched her hand away.

At the top the polished wood floor and strip of carpet stretched away forever. *Lew!* Jo strained to run. Her feet might have been cast from lead.

A hand grabbed hers and pulled. Calvin was running beside her, leaning nearly horizontal in the effort to make headway against whatever was holding them back.

The end of the corridor shrank slowly, slowly toward them. The morning glory lights on the walls dimmed and died as they passed. The last door on the left was open. A dead white light shone from it. You'd think the moon was trapped in there.

And I promised him he'd be safe!

The grip of Calvin's hand was warm and real — the only good and normal thing in Jo's world. It gave her strength. She flung herself forward, flew the last few metres, crashed into the end wall. Gasping with pain, she grabbed the doorframe and swung herself around. She fell inside. And stopped.

A slender figure in white bent over Lew's bed. Its radiance bleached everything in the room. A nurse, Jo thought. She — it — it's a nurse.

The nurse put Lew's cover aside. She gathered him up into her arms with a strong, gentle motion. She stood there holding him and looking down into his face. His eyes were closed. It's all right, Jo thought. It must be all right. She's so loving, so gentle.

She slumped against the wall. A sleepy warmth seeped through her, a reaction to the violent effort of climbing and running, and the fear and desperation. Calvin stepped in beside her, and she put out a hand to hold him back. Everything was going to be all right now.

And then the nurse turned, and looked at her, and Jo saw the eyes, holes of darkness in a moon-white mask. She backed away and raised a hand against that famished gaze. With the other hand she felt behind her for the doorframe.

Got to get out. Got to get out. I can't let it touch me again!

She wasn't sure, later, what she would have done if Lew hadn't made that sound. Like a kitten, or a small bird, something very young and lost, crying. It broke the shell of terror around her. For that moment she could move.

She threw herself at the shining white figure, head down. It was like diving into a pool of icy water. Blinding whiteness closed around her. In its heart was something small and alive. She wrapped herself around the small living thing and dropped into darkness.

Chapter 21

THE VOICES CAME from far away. ...*happened,* someone said, and
...*ambulance...*

"The nearest hospital is in Burfast." Calvin's voice was suddenly
near and clear. "We'll have to take him ourselves."

Jo opened her eyes. She was lying on the stone floor next to
Lew's bed. Lew was cradled in her arms. His eyes were still closed.
She touched his throat under one ear. Then struggled to sit up.

"He's... his heart, it's not..."

"It's beating. Not very strong." Calvin scooped Lew out of her
arms. "Glad you woke up. I was afraid I'd have to pry him away from
you with a crowbar. C'mon."

She staggered to her feet. He was already out the door. She ran
after him along the gallery to the stairs. "What happened?"

"Later." He stepped carefully down the stairs, holding his burden
close. "If Mel's done her job and not fallen to pieces, she's phoned
for an ambulance and told them to look for us. We'll be coming along
the highway with our flashers on."

The next hour was a blur. It took Mel and Jo working together to
wake up Frieda and persuade her into the car. She kept asking bewildered questions and not hearing the answers. She only fell silent
when she was settled in the back seat next to Jo with Lew, wrapped
in a blanket, lying like a package across both their laps.

Mel, sitting beside Calvin in the front, wiped tears from her face.
"Jo?"

"Yeah?"

"You're all right?"

Jo shivered. "I'm okay now." After a few deep breaths she said, "Are you? All right?"

"N- no." Mel covered her face with both hands.

The ambulance met the station wagon halfway and Lew was transferred from one vehicle to the other. Frieda, who had been growing more alert and anxious with each mile that separated her from Spinbrook House, climbed into the back of the ambulance with Lew. The station wagon followed behind.

Mel huddled down in the front seat with beams from the ambulance's whirling light skipping across her face. "I've been so afraid," she quavered. "Of myself. That's my secret fear. "I'm af- afraid of what I'm turning into."

"That wasn't you in Lew's room," Calvin said. "You were downstairs."

"I was asleep. And then, all of a sudden, I was in the water. In the dark and the cold. And it — it wasn't a dream. It was real."

"Mel, you weren't in any water," Jo said. "You couldn't have been. You'd be wet."

"I was in the water," Mel insisted. "I was floating. And then, all of a sudden, I was lying on that stone floor in the cellar. So cold…" She hugged herself. "And, Jo, it — it wasn't the first time."

"How many times?" Calvin asked, matter-of-factly.

Mel wiped her face and thought about it. Calvin's approach seemed the best one to take, Jo thought. Mel let out a long sigh. "At first, after I got here, it was about every third night. Then every second night. This last week, it's been every night."

And Lew had been getting sicker and weaker, night by night.

Jo said nothing. Whatever had walked up those stairs ahead of her had looked like Mel. But it hadn't been Mel. What had the invisible writer said? *It needs to be invited in.... Would one of the Sisters be doing it? Not on purpose... But what might happen in dreams?*

A LITTLE AFTER three in the morning, Jo woke to find someone shaking her. She sat up and blinked around at the beige walls and brown vinyl-covered furniture. Where were her sheets and pillow? Where was her bedroom? Was this another dream?

"Jo!"

At the sight of Frieda's face above her, memory clicked in. This was the waiting room in Burfast Hospital. Mel was curled up against her on the couch, still asleep. Calvin, slumped in a chair nearby, pulled in his long legs from their stretch and rubbed his eyes.

Frieda knelt down so her eyes were level with Jo's. "I thought you'd want to know."

"Lew?" Jo grabbed at her arm.

"He's going to pull through." She looked exhausted, but fully alive. A different woman, Jo thought. A lot less chipper but more intelligent. "His condition is still serious, but he'll survive."

"I'm so glad!"

"I want to say… thank you." She held Jo's hands, then looked at Calvin, who nodded back at her solemnly. Then she stood up and smiled at Mel, who was still sleeping. "I've phoned Harold in San Diego and he's flying back. Until he gets here I'll be staying in Lew's room here in the hospital. But you three should go home in the morning."

"Home," Jo murmured, after Frieda had left.

So," Calvin said. "You're leaving?"

Jo thought of her own crowded, noisy urban neighbourhood. She ached to be there, where the world behaved the way it was supposed to, and night was never dark, never something to be afraid of. And where people wore their own faces, friendly or not, and there wasn't anything monstrous lurking beneath.

She sat up straight and shook her head. "Not yet. Because Mel can't go home yet. I guess I better stay until she can." She sent Calvin a smile. "At least things will be getting back to normal now. Or soon will be."

"Think so?"

"Well, sure. Lew's going to be okay… Right?" She rubbed her arms, suddenly cold all over. She began to shake. "Calvin, what… what did you see when… when I…"

"Hold on." He walked out of the waiting room and was back in two minutes with a blanket. He tucked it around her and went out again. Next time he came back, he carried a cardboard cup that steamed.

"Th— th— thank—" Jo managed.

"Drink up. It's vending machine cocoa, so it's sure to be fairly crappy, but at least it's hot."

Jo sipped at the hot, syrupy drink and felt a little better. She felt better still when Calvin wrapped an arm around her blanketed shoulders. Warm and safe. Safe enough to try to be brave.

"Calvin. What did you see when I tackled that thing?"

"I saw…" He took a deep breath and for a moment his arm around Jo's shoulders tightened. "I saw it smile at you."

She tried to laugh, and shuddered instead. She thought of those hungry, empty eyes.

"Jo," Calvin said softly, "I think you better go home. I mean, really home. I can stay with Mel. I live here, you don't."

"No, I'm staying."

"Pig-headed, much?"

"Maybe. But I told you before, I don't run out on my friends."

"Yes, but Jo... It's already touched you twice. I think it wants you."

THEY FELL ASLEEP, the three of them in an untidy row on the couch, and woke in the morning, stiff and sore. Sunlight poured in through the waiting room windows. Hunger drove them to the hospital's cafeteria, where they found a good, hot buffet breakfast, and Frieda, and news. "Lew's heart is much stronger," she announced, smiling over her coffee cup. "If he keeps on improving like this, we may be able to bring him home in a week."

"A week!" Jo lowered her juice glass and met Mel's startled eyes. "Why, that's — "

"That's just wonderful," Mel said flatly.

Calvin swallowed a mouthful of ham-and-egg and set down his fork. "Are you planning to take Lew away on holiday?"

"We'll see. Perhaps, if he's strong enough. Harold will be here later today and we'll discuss it. By the way, Harold and I will be staying in a motel here in Burfast while Lew is in hospital. If you need us, it's the Riverview. I think you all know my cell phone number." She looked around the table. "Jo and Mel, you'll be all right by yourselves at the house, won't you?"

"Oh, sure." Jo forced a smile. "We'll be fine."

"Mel, your parents are due back from Australia in another what, ten days? But feel free to stay at Spinbrook House until school starts, if you like. And Jo, please stay for as long as you need, and forget the fee. You're a good friend now."

"Thanks. That's so nice of you." Jo wished she could sound more enthusiastic.

"It's the least I can do." Lew's mother got up from the table and touched Jo's shoulder. "I don't know what I would have done last night without you. All of you."

They watched her thread her way energetically between the tables. The room was filling up with people and conversation and the smell of coffee and toast.

"A week," Mel said. "A week and he's home again."

Jo picked up a croissant and put it down again. She had lost her appetite. "Last night I thought we'd won and it was all over. I thought Lew was safe, because we got him taken away. But he's not."

"But if they take him away on holiday," Mel began.

"If they do, it's a breathing space," Calvin cut in. "But sooner or later they'll bring him back to Spinbrook House. And none of us will be around then to protect him. Not that we've done such a great job so far."

"And *it* will still be here," Jo said.

"That's right. It won't go away. It won't get tired of waiting. It knows how to wait."

Mel looked from face to face as her own cheeks whitened. "What are we going to do?"

Chapter 22

BEFORE HEADING BACK to Spinbrook House they shopped for groceries in a supermarket on Burfast's main street. It felt unreal, Jo thought, to be deciding between whole wheat and multigrain bread, sliced or unsliced, after what she'd seen and done and felt in the last twenty-four hours.

"And we'll need milk and butter," Mel said brightly. "And juice. Oh, and frozen waffles, for sure."

Her brightness faded as they belted themselves into the station wagon. "This is ridiculous," she muttered. "We should be driving top speed the other way, not back to that crazy house."

"We'll be okay," Jo said. "I just wish we could be sure Lew will be okay. I wish there was something we could do to keep him safe!"

"We can't do anything." Mel, in the back seat, glowered out at the green woods and sunny fields. It was a beautiful day. "Because we don't know anything. You can't fight what you don't know."

"But we all know some things." Jo lifted her head. "Yes! I just realized. All of us — you, me, Calvin — each of us has... touched... it." She shivered, then forged ahead. "So each of us should know something. Maybe if we put together all the bits of what we know, no matter how small, we'll be able to figure out..." She waved a hand helplessly.

"What?" Mel demanded. "How to destroy it? Dream on!"

"I don't think it's something that can be destroyed," Calvin said, his eyes on the road.

"Right, and I bet your great-granddad Jeremy knew that," Mel said morosely. "I bet that's why he burned down the orphanage. He knew there was no way to keep *it* away from the kids, so he made sure the kids would be kept away from *it*."

"There's one thing we know, anyway," Jo said. "Based on what we feel as we go away."

"The way the threat lifts?" Calvin drummed his forefingers on the steering wheel.

"Right. It can't follow. It must be tied to that spot. There's got to be some way we can use that."

"We can't burn down Spinbrook House!" Mel sounded shocked. Then, thoughtfully: "Can we?"

"It would work for a while," Calvin said, as they turned from the highway onto the gravel drive. "But it wouldn't work forever, because..."

As the car came out from under the trees, the house lay before them like some big, graceful animal, its stone frame and cedar shingles melting into the surrounding woods, its windows like wide-awake eyes.

"Because someone else would come here, and build another house," Jo finished for him.

"That's right. There will always be someone else, someone who doesn't know." Calvin studied the house. "Someone with children. Who thinks this is the perfect spot to raise a family."

"Or maybe not a house. Maybe a campground. Beautiful spot to camp out with the kids."

They carried the groceries into the kitchen. As they unpacked them and put them away, Mel paused, cereal box in hand. Her face lit up. "Dynamite!"

Calvin shook his head. "I know what you're thinking. Dynamite the stream and change its course, right?"

"Yes! It could work!"

"No. We might even blast the pool deeper. And even if we didn't, there would still be dark pools somewhere along the stream."

"Sounds like you've thought about this a lot," Jo said. "How come you're so sure?"

"I've had years to think about it."

"Then you must understand it much better than Mel or me. And you've put all that in your pictures. Am I right?"

He shoved the last of the boxes and cans in a cupboard and turned around, looking glumly resigned. "Okay, you win. Come see."

CALVIN'S ROOM above the garage was big and bare and smelled of acrylic paint. The walls were enamelled white. It contained the minimum of furniture: a single bed covered with a log cabin quilt, a battered-looking chest of drawers, a built-in closet with a mirror on the door, a wooden kitchen chair and a small paint-stained table.

The paintings stood in a row along one wall, their faces turned inward. They were not large, none more than a metre high, and all done on masonite or plywood. "I cadge scraps from Kyle and my dad." He shrugged. "Stretched canvas is expensive."

Jo pulled open the curtains to let the sunshine in. "How come you don't hang these on the walls?" She picked up the nearest painting and turned it around, and froze. Ice crept up her spine. Calvin sat on the bed, elbows on knees, and watched.

Mel took one look, then turned her back and gazed out the window.

"You sure do have a gift," Jo said. "But I can see why you don't let your mom and dad see things like this."

The painting showed the dark pool below the falls. Close under the surface, a face looked up. It was death-like and barely human, pale green through the lens of the water.

Now it seemed to her that the face in the pool was looking back at her. Smiling faintly. She set the painting down carefully and stepped away from it. Turned another one around.

This one showed the waterfall. The white cascade was a woman's flowing dress. The rocks formed a sweet face with a hungry smile. A white hand curled and beckoned.

Jo turned the paintings back to face the wall. "What is this thing?"

"I did some reading, the last couple of years," said Calvin from the bed. "Ever heard of Jenny Greenteeth? Or Peg Powler? No? Those are from English folklore. They're a kind of hag that lives in dangerous pools. They grab people by the ankles — young kids, especially — and drag them down to drown."

"Lovely!" Mel muttered.

"Oh, I know how stories like that get started," Jo said lightly. She looked at another painting without really seeing it. "They were invented to keep kids from danger. Parents would say to their kids, 'Don't you play near that pool, or Peg Powler will get you!'"

"The bogeyman strategy," Mel said over her shoulder. "Scare them to keep them safe."

"Right," Calvin said. "Only, suppose it's not just a story? Suppose it's real?"

Jo set the painting down and picked up another, handling it carefully by the edges. It still smelled of damp paint. "Does folklore give us any hints on how to deal with this hag, or whatever it is?"

"Stay away from dark pools."

"That's not very helpful, not when it can come right in the house." She glanced at the picture she was holding. Then really looked at it.

Mel turned to look too. Then she let out a cry and threw herself at the door. She was clattering down the stairs before Jo and Calvin were out on the landing.

Chapter 23

"MEL!" JO SHOUTED. "Come back!" But Mel didn't stop. In a few seconds she had vanished inside the house. Jo shoved the painting at Calvin and raced down the stairs after her. When she reached the house Mel was shut in her bedroom with the door locked.

"It isn't you — not really!" Jo called through the door.

Mel didn't answer. After a few minutes of pleading and reassuring, all of it one-sided, Jo went back to the room over the garage. Calvin was sitting on the bed again. Jo leaned on the chest of drawers and pointed at the picture that was still damp.

"Is that your latest?"

"Yep. Did it yesterday. I told you I paint my nightmares." Calvin nodded at the painting, which stood under the window facing them. "That was in my nightmare."

In the painting, a figure dressed in shining white stood halfway up a staircase, looking out at the viewer over the railing. A pale hand curled around the balustrade. The fingers were disturbingly long and thin, and sharply pointed. The face, framed in hair as fine and white as cloud, was Mel's — except for the eyes.

And there was more. Jo didn't want to touch the picture, but she made herself pick it up and hold it up to the brighter light near the window. "You've got Lew's face in there too, down in the shadows. And Frieda's face sort of in the swirls of the hair... and...." She held it closer and squinted. "Back there... can't quite make it out... is that me?" Her stomach went cold.

Calvin nodded. "You'll find lots more if you look," he said, as if that was encouraging. "I'm in there. And that boy in the photo Sister Jerome showed us, he's there too."

She looked again. "So he is. That's amazing. Why...?"

"I think they're all people it's touched."

"Frieda? But — "

"It touched her. It must have."

Jo turned the painting's face to the wall. "I thought you said it only wants the young ones."

"Well, she's not sick, is she? But it did something to her, all right."

"The not-seeing? The sunny optimism?"

"Yeah."

"And Mel..." Jo took a breath. "It used her to get in. I think it must have been using her ever since she got here." She told Calvin what the invisible writer had said, about *it* needing to be invited into a human house. "But Lew started getting sick when they first arrived here, a year ago. Mel wasn't here then."

"So it must have started by using Mrs. Stone."

"Then why switch to Mel?"

"Easier, maybe? Because she's younger? Mel's still a kid, really."

Jo nodded. "That would explain why Lew got so much worse this summer. Mel was easier to use." She turned the painting to the wall. "I wonder what it was before it sucked in all those people, or bits of people. When did it begin? Where did it come from?"

"You ask darn good questions. I wish I had some answers. And now..." He slid off the bed and stepped to the door. Jo followed him out.

"Where are you going?"

"To the shed."

"What's there?"

"Hedge clippers, rake, lawn mower. Mrs. Stone pays me to keep the place nice. So that's what I'm going to do."

JO DECIDED Calvin was taking the right tack — getting back to normal. It wasn't easy, with Mel locked in her room, but Jo tried. She had a shower and then dressed in clean shorts and her favourite red-and-white T-shirt. The day was turning hot. She sat on the terrace outside her room to write a carefully worded letter to her parents. A curtain on Mel's window twitched once, the only sign that she was still in there.

Jo wrote several pages in her journal, and was disappointed when the opposite page stayed blank.

"Maybe that means it's really over," she told Calvin as they sat at the kitchen table at noon, eating cheese and tomato sandwiches. "If my invisible helper has gone away."

"Yeah, maybe." He didn't sound convinced.

Jo had knocked on Mel's door and left a wrapped sandwich and a glass of milk on the floor outside. She checked on Mel again after lunch, and found the sandwich gone and the glass emptied. At least she wasn't wasting away in there. Jo knocked on the door again. A muffled voice told her to go away.

"Mel, it's not only you in that painting. It's everybody it touched, Calvin and me included. You're just one of us."

"But I'm the main one!"

"That doesn't mean — "

"Go away!"

Jo sighed and carried the glass downstairs to the kitchen. No more room service, she decided. Mel would have to come out sooner or later.

In the living room she stood looking around and listening. The house drowsed in the sun. Outside the stream glittered, sending golden spangles through the windows to dance on the ceiling. A breath of warm, cut-grass-scented air drifted through the house along with the soft clatter of the lawn mower's revolving blades. Everything was perfect. Even the constant, almost forgotten roar of the waterfall was sleepy-soft, like a cat's purr. Hard to believe such a thing as Peg Powler existed on a day like this.

"We shouldn't be moping around inside," Jo announced to the room. "We should be out soaking up the sun."

She glanced upward, considered trying to dig Mel out one more time, and decided to save her breath. Grabbing a bottle of spring water from the kitchen, she headed out into the sunshine. For the next two hours she followed the trails in the woods on the far side of the highway.

By the time she came tramping back, tired, sweaty and somewhere close to calm, she was ready for a nap. She dropped onto the leather sofa in front of the empty fireplace and yawned. This was what came of sleeping on a couch in a hospital waiting room... Could fall asleep now... so... easily...

Her eyes closed. In the dark behind the lids, a green-white blotch floated like the after-image of a photo flash. Or like an oval face, glowing softly through water, smiling gently. Face from one of Calvin's paintings. Not so scary after all... beautiful...

A freezing touch on one foot shocked her awake. She had slumped and slid down the slick leather, and lay with her legs stretched out, her feet close to the hearthstone. One toe had brushed the stone.

"Wow, that thing is cold!" She sat up and looked at the stone. It sparkled in the bright light flooding through the windows. Crystals in the stone, she thought. And looked again, and reached to brush a finger across the rough granite. It wasn't just cold. It was coated with frost. She stared at the particles melting on her fingertip. Frost, on an August afternoon.

She backed away from the hearthstone, shaking her hand to send the icy droplets flying. *I've got to get out of this house!* She started for the door, then thought of Mel and raced up the stairs.

"Mel!" She pounded on the bedroom door.

No answer.

"Mel, listen to me! I think it's getting stronger. We need to leave the house now!"

Silence. Jo rattled the doorknob in frustration and the door swung open. She looked in. "Mel?" No Mel. And, as she discovered after crossing the room to the window, no Mel on the terrace, either.

Turning back from the window, she saw the piece of paper lying on the bedspread. She picked it up. It was a note in Mel's curly handwriting.

I can't stay here any more. Don't worry about me — I'll go to Etobicoke. I have a friend there I can stay with. Jo, please take care of Lew. And take care of yourself too, okay? Mel.

Chapter 24

"SHE CAN'T BE taking the bus," Calvin said. "It doesn't come through MacPhee until evening."

"Then she's planning to hitchhike. The idiot!" Jo stared along the highway as it unreeled toward them, hoping to spot a familiar thin figure walking along the shoulder.

"She must be desperate. If only she'd told me, I could have given her a lift, or... There she is!" He slowed down and put on his flashers. As the car came level with Mel she glanced back once, then kept on marching, eyes front.

Jo hung out the passenger side window. "Mel, you've got to be kidding!"

Mel jerked her head from side to side.

"Are you crazy, hitchhiking? Don't you know how dangerous that can be?"

"Not as dangerous as staying in that house." Mel yanked up the straps of her backpack and marched on.

"Stop," Jo said to Calvin. "Let me out." She jumped out before the car had stopped moving, caught up to Mel and matched her stride for stride.

"Don't waste your time," Mel said. "I'm not going back there."

"What about Lew, then?"

Mel stopped short and faced around. "I can't help Lew. I can't help anybody." She threw her hands in the air. "Don't you get it? I was the one who... who..."

"Who let the thing in? Yeah, we figured that out."

Mel stared. "Aren't you scared of me? *I'm* scared of me."

Jo opened her mouth to say *Oh, don't be silly*. Then knew this was no time for reassuring lies. "Yes, I am. A bit. About as much as I'm afraid of Calvin, or Lew. We've all lost a bit of ourselves to that thing. That probably means we all have a bit of it in us. And that means me, too." *A touch of darkness*. "I keep thinking we should be able to use that, somehow."

"I don't see how." Mel turned and walked on. "Anyway, I can't do any good and I've messed up enough. I don't want to turn into… into something worse. I won't go back!"

"Okay, if you really have to leave, at least don't hitch. Let Calvin drive you."

"Better yet," he called over the noise of the engine, "stay at my place." Mel stopped again and frowned at him through the window. He braked the car. "I know my parents would be glad to put you up for a few days," he went on matter-of-factly. "You could stay in my room, since I'm not in it right now. You'd be safe there."

Mel looked down at her dusty sandals, then up at Calvin, still frowning. "Why aren't you leaving?"

Calvin glanced at Jo. "Because she isn't."

Jo felt a sudden warm pang. "Really?"

Calvin looked away. Pink touched his cheekbones. *He's blushing!* Jo did a gleeful dance in the private chamber of her mind.

"Huh." Mel was not impressed. "And, Jo, why…"

Jo shook her head. "I'd be running out on Lew. I need to be there when he comes back. I promised to keep him safe once, and I broke my promise, and I have to make up for that. Yes, I know, none of that's rational. That's the way it is."

Mel closed her eyes tight, then opened them. "You win. I'll stay. And, no, not with your parents, Calvin. Thanks for the offer, but I'd feel like such a wimp if I hid out there while the two of you stayed at Spinbrook House. I'd never hold up my head again." She threw her pack into the back seat of the station wagon and climbed in after it. "Promise me one thing, Jo. No, two things."

"What?"

"Promise me we'll stay together at night, okay? And if I make one move toward the cellar stairs, tie me up and sit on me!"

"THERE'S ONE THING we know," Jo said, as they sat on the lawn at sunset eating microwaved pizza. "It likes to get its victims alone. It tackles them one at a time. So that means we should all stick together. Including you, Calvin."

"No way. I have a painting I need to work on."

"A painting!" Mel stared at him, incredulous. "You want to paint? Now?"

"Oh," Jo said. "You mean… one of those…"

"Yep, one of those. I'm always hoping it will be the last one I'll have to do."

"I don't understand. I thought you liked doing them."

"Like doing them? Are you kidding? They…" He took a bite of pizza, chewed and swallowed. "They're a kind of pressure valve, I guess. The nightmares build up in here." He tapped his chest in the region of his heart. "The painting's like a door to let them out. After I get one done I feel better. The nightmares stop. For a while, anyway. I'm always hoping some day I'll do one that will capture the thing once and for all, and I'll be rid of it. And then no more nightmares."

After a moment of thoughtful silence Jo said, "Why not bring your painting to the house?"

"That's right," Mel said. "The more the merrier."

Calvin took another bite of pizza and didn't answer. But when it grew dark, he carried a large rectangle of masonite to the house, along with a box of paint tubes, brushes, rags, and other gear. He spread sheets of newspaper over a kitchen chair, propped the masonite against the chair back and started work, but wouldn't let anyone look. "No previews allowed!" he said, when Mel tried to lean in behind him.

Melanie and Jo watched television in the living room until Jo grew tired of seeing Mel glance, again and again, toward the cellar stairs. And tired of her own impulse to go over and feel the hearthstone, which had been cool to the touch, not frosty, since they'd returned. She went up to her room to write in her journal. Mel went with her and curled up on the bed with a fashion magazine while Jo sat at the desk.

It looks like we've got it beat, at least for now, she wrote. *We're sticking together, and probably it won't want us, anyway. We're too old. I hope.*

She paused uneasily, thinking of the dark pool and the icy grip on her ankle. It wanted me then, she thought.

But that doesn't do Lew any good. We have to think of a permanent solution. I wish...

She stopped writing and sat back. "Mel!" Mel slid off the bed and peered over Jo's shoulder. She clapped a hand to her mouth. Angular handwriting scratched across the right-hand page.

...fight ice with fire. That may be the only way we can save the young ones. Marie has thought of a way to queer its pitch it once and for all, but that's beyond us. She says the thing's heart, its stronghold, must be under....

The writing broke off, then began again. Blue ink spattered as the spiky handwriting ran across the page. He was writing fast, cramming the words down, skipping any marks not needed. *Its coming, I feel it, its coming here. I think it knows I mean to end it — that lights coming under the door — got to keep writing longs I can so Marie knows — the door opens it looks like*

The writing broke off. Ink drops trailed across the page, as if the pen had dropped and rolled. Then it faded, writing, drops, and all.

Jo grabbed her gel pen and wrote randomly, scribbling anything that came into her head. But the invisible writer never came back. After five minutes she threw down her pen and closed the journal with a bang. "What do you think? Did he survive?"

"Who knows?" Mel was back on the bed. She had crawled under the coverlet despite the warmth of the night and pulled it up around her head. "But it shows: it doesn't want only the young ones. He was obviously at least in his mid-teens — like me — and it came after him."

"We don't know for sure that it got him," Jo said. "Maybe he got the hell out of there. I hope so."

"I hope so, too. But..." Mel freed a hand from the coverlet and pointed at the door. "Lock that, will you? I'm not leaving this room till morning."

Jo turned the thumb latch, thinking that a lock wasn't going to stop this thing. She left the room one more time: went down to the kitchen to persuade Calvin to abandon his painting. "You can sleep in my room too. Get your sleeping bag — or better yet, we'll drag the mattress in from Mel's bed and you can stretch out inside the door."

"Like the faithful hound?" He grinned, but didn't stop painting. She edged around to peek at the picture. He gave her a stern look and she backed off.

"Think this one will do it for you?"

"I hope. Got a feeling about it... I'm not stopping now. You go to bed, I'll be fine."

"Bring it upstairs. Set it up in the bedroom."

He paused, brush poised, eyebrows raised.

"I mean it. None of us should be alone tonight. I've got a feeling."

She thought he was going to shrug her off. Then he nodded and gathered his supplies. Upstairs, while Mel complained about the smell of fresh paint, he spread newspaper on the desk chair and propped the painting up on it with its back to the bed. After Jo turned off the overhead lights, Calvin aimed the desk lamp at the painting. He arranged his box of paints and his palette on another sheet of newspaper on the floor beside him, knelt down in front of the chair, and got back to work.

The last thing Jo saw before she fell asleep was Calvin's intent face lit by the lamplight that bounced off the painting. She thought: I hope he captures it this time. I hope this one ends his nightmares.

OUT OF CONFUSED dreams of running and searching, Jo woke to a dead stillness. Her ears felt numb. The room was dark, except for a light reflecting off the wall she was facing. The light came from somewhere behind her. She couldn't see Calvin, but he must still be painting.

But if he was, he wasn't making a sound. Not even the soft scuff of brush bristles on board.

He must have fallen asleep with the light on, she told herself as she turned over, carefully, so as not to wake Mel. But no, there he was, kneeling in front of the chair with his brush in the air. It seemed he had stopped at that moment to gaze at his work. He didn't look happy with it. His face, what she could see of it behind the painting, looked frozen, the mouth drawn down.

"Calvin?" she whispered. Her heart thudded.

The light from the desk lamp dimmed, went brown and died. Darkness closed in from the corners of the room. Jo groped for her bedside lamp and clicked it on. The bulb shone brightly. Then it yellowed, browned, faded to nothing. Darkness again, thick as smoke. Jo struggled to breathe.

"Cal – Calvin?"

Slowly his face grew brighter. A light was shining on him, but not from the desk lamp. The light shone from the painting, a cold white light that grew colder as it brightened.

"Calvin!" She crashed out of bed, landing on her hands and knees. "Calvin, get away from there!" Behind her, Mel flung the covers into the air.

He didn't move. Jo knocked over the chair. The painting fell to the floor, face down. She grabbed Calvin by the arm and hauled at him. He looked up at her, bewildered. "Get away!" she shouted.

"But... what..."

"Look!" She pointed at the painting on the floor. Calvin made a noise and reached for it, then pulled his hand back. The only light in the room came from there. Dead white light oozed from under it and rose like wisps of fog. The wisps drifted together. They began to form a shape.

Chapter 25

THEY DIDN'T STOP to see what shape would form. They ran, with Calvin a step behind Jo. Mel was already halfway down the stairs when they reached the stair head. As they burst out the front door onto the lawn, she was within two strides of the woods to the east. Moonlight lit her flying hair. Next moment she was gone.

"Mel! Not that way!" Jo started after her, but Calvin caught her arm.

"She'll be okay. Look there!"

Jo looked back at the house. Every window, upstairs and down, glowed with a light like snow. "What's happening?"

"I don't know, but I wouldn't go back in there for a million bucks." His face in the moonlight was all white crests and black hollows. "The painting, though. I think I got it right, this time."

"You must have. It couldn't get in by using one of us, so it used your painting — just like the picture was a person, not paint. Too bad you couldn't have destroyed the picture right then, with the thing halfway in and halfway out."

"Don't know if that would've done any good."

The glow in the house dimmed. The blank windows winked back at the moon. "What do we..." Jo began, and broke off at a cry from the woods near the ravine. "That's Mel!" She was off and running before Calvin could stop her.

She hadn't taken more than a dozen steps inside the woods before she realized her mistake. You couldn't charge through a moonlit forest at night, not even a normal, natural forest, with its patchwork of intense black and glaring silver, and expect to find anything but scrapes and bruises. And this forest was far from normal and natural. After the first headlong spill into a tangle of prickly brush, she picked herself up and felt her way along gingerly on bare feet, step by step, tree trunk by trunk. By then she no longer knew where to look for Mel.

She called. Voices answered, echoey and far away, with no clear direction. Then the ceaseless music of flowing water swelled. The ground grew steep under her feet. She grabbed at a branch for support.

Now she knew where she was: on the hillside near the falls. The house had to be very near.

"Mel!" she called. No answer. Then a patch of silver moved between the trees below. As it came nearer, it took shape. Someone's head... Jo's breath came short and her heart pounded.

When Calvin stepped into view, she laughed with relief. His flaxen hair shone in the moonlight. "You! For a minute I thought it was — You know."

He stood watching her with a strange look in his eyes. Then he came toward her, his hands held out, his face a question. Jo's heart pounded again: this time, not from fear. His arms slipped around her and she felt a moment of happy warmth. She closed her eyes.

One moment, and the warmth changed to cold, and the cold to ice, thick and paralyzing. She tried to break free, to call out, but could not move or make a sound. She opened her eyes and looked up into Calvin's face. There was only darkness.

SOMETHING INVISIBLE and horribly strong was dragging Jo down the hill. She fought, grabbed at tree trunks with icy hands, dug her bare heels into half-frozen earth, but step by step she lurched downward. Every step took her closer to the dark pool below the waterfall. The noise of the falls sounded like a huge animal roaring in pain.

"Help me!" she screamed, and knew she'd made no sound.

At the edge of the trees near the pool she wrapped her arms around a slim birch, then hooked one leg around it and got the tree between her and the pull. The pressure squashed the air from her chest. *Hold on. Hold... on...*

The tree was leafless. The woods were black and white. That was winter, not moonlight. It wasn't night — somehow she knew that — but a cold white light, like starlight reflected from snow, pervaded everything. The pool was black as tar, except where ice crusted its margins and patched the little inlets.

Other people were caught in the same pull that had dragged her this far. Small figures: children, mostly. But unlike her, they didn't struggle. They drifted like ghosts down the hill and across the rocks and ice patches and into the water. They slid down into the pool, feet first, heads last, as if they were being sucked down. A circle of foam revolving on the surface marked where each had vanished.

After watching for a while, Jo noticed something else happening. With each new victim the pool sucked in, the water inched higher up the rocks.

Not all of them went quietly. Here came a fighter, this small shape sliding backward down the hill toward her. It was down on its hands and knees, grabbing at shrubs and rocks and losing them, scraping gouges out of the earth with its feet. It was almost past when Jo bent sideways from her tree, still with one arm and both legs wrapped around the trunk, reached out with the other hand and grabbed the child by the back of his T-shirt.

The child latched onto her arm with both hands and dug in with his toes. She pulled with all her strength, and he pulled, and next moment he was beside her. They clung to each other and to the tree, and the drag of the dark pool was suddenly less.

We made a difference by joining our strength! We can resist! She felt a flare of hope.

The boy looked up at her out of big, startled dark eyes.

"Lew?"

"Well, sort of."

"What do you mean?"

"See those others?" Lew pointed. Another unresisting figure slid into the pool. A finger of water inched between the rocks at the edge and ran across the ground nearly to Jo's foot. "They're making the pool grow, so it can get you." He looked up at her solemnly. "We're the ones it really wants: you, me, Mel, and Calvin."

"Why us?"

"Because we're alive. See? It only got a part of us, and it really, really wants the other part. All those others — " He nodded toward the pool. "They're just ghosts, they can't do anything. But we still can."

"Like what? What can we do?"

Lew sighed with exaggerated patience. "We can get out of here. Only, we better do it soon, or it will get all of you. And then you'll be a ghost too."

The water touched her right foot. Her toes went numb. She pulled the foot back.

"Okay, you're right. But what about him?"

A metre away, on the edge of the pool, a small curly-haired child stood looking down at the ice-patched water. She hadn't noticed him before. Unlike the others, he seemed to feel no pull. And he looked solid and unghostly enough. He was dressed in heavy, dark clothing

— like the children in Sister Jerome's photograph, Jo remembered. He reached out one booted foot and tested the crust of ice beside the shore. A hand-sized red-and white object lay on the ice. A toy soldier. If he'd laid down flat it would have been an inch or two beyond his reach.

"Leave it!" Jo called. "Come away from there!"

"Don't bother with him!" Lew tried to pull Jo away from the tree, back up the hill.

"But look at him! He must be alive, like us! We have to save him!"

"No! Don't you see — "

"Don't!" Jo screamed. The curly-haired boy had taken a careful step onto the ice. A second step, and he broke through to his waist. He cried out.

"You keep hold of the tree," Jo said. Then she let go of the tree herself and lunged toward the boy in the water. He grabbed her outstretched arms. His grip around her wrists was icy-cold. And far too strong. His round, young face tilted up at her and where his eyes should have been were pits of darkness.

Someone yelled "Jo!" behind her.

The boy sank down into the pool, pulling Jo after him. She sprawled flat on the slushy ground and dug in with her toes.

Small hands seized her ankles and tugged backward, but did no good.

With all her strength she twisted her right arm free and locked it around a rock at the edge of the pool. The surface of the water was an inch under her nose. At the end of her straining left arm, a face stared up at her through the dark water. Not a child's face, not any more. She shut her eyes tight.

Hold on. Hold on. Her arm ached. Her shoulder creaked. *Can't hold out much longer.* "Calvin, help! Help!"

Hands pried at her hold on the rock.

"No! Can't let go!"

"Jo, you have to let go now. Let go of the rock, Jo. Let go of the rock!"

"JO. LET GO of the rock. Let go of the rock, Jo." The voice was familiar. Strong hands pried her arm away from the stone. Then the world swung around her. She was being carried. She kept her eyes closed and nestled her head against a warm, yielding, spicy-smelling surface. Something thumped under her right ear. Lub-dup, lub-dup. A heartbeat.

She opened her eyes once to see Mel running ahead through the moonlight, opening the front door of the house. She opened her eyes again when her body settled onto something soft. It was the leather sofa in the living room, in front of the empty fireplace. She shuddered with cold and wrapped her arms around herself, missing Calvin's warmth.

Fragment followed fragment. A thick woolly blanket tucked in around her. Shivers rippling through her like wind through tall grass. Calvin's voice: "She's like a block of ice!" The aroma of tea tickling her nose. Mel kneeling in front of her, her eyes big and anxious above a steaming cup.

Fire leaped in the fireplace. Calvin hacked at something with an axe and threw the pieces onto the fire. As it splintered and broke Jo saw it was a painting. A face looked out at her from the flames.

"It's you," she mumbled. "You painted yourself. That's how...."

She drifted into bad dreams.

Chapter 26

JO LAY ON A blanket on the lawn in front of the house and tilted back her head to let the sun warm her throat. It was mid-afternoon. She had been out there, in shorts and tank top, for most of the day, too cold to stay inside the cool stony house, at first too weak even to walk. She nursed cups of hot tea and tried to keep her eyes open. Every time she closed them she saw a lovely, sweet, terrible face that kept changing into other faces — strange children's faces, and Mel's, and even Calvin's — only, not the Mel and Calvin she knew.

The only thing that made her feel stronger was being in the sun. Hour by hour, under its healing touch, life and energy crept back into her body.

"This … um, vision of yours," Calvin said thoughtfully. He was sitting on the grass beside her blanket, sketching on a pad of thick paper. A box of charcoal sticks bulged the pocket of his blue cotton shirt. Mel, wearing her scarlet swimsuit, was stretched out on another blanket nearby, sunning her back.

Funny! Jo thought. To look at, they were just a bunch of friends hanging out. No cares, no problems, no thoughts more worrisome than *Does he really like me?* Which was worrisome enough!

"Not a vision," she said. "It was real. Lew said we four were the only ones who could do anything in that place, because we were the ones who were alive."

"And the other kid...." He went on sketching. The face taking shape on the page was round and young, seven or eight years old. Fine dark hair curled around it, floating, as if lifted by water.

"Who's that?" Jo asked, but she knew.

"It came to me when you talked about what you saw last night."

"You haven't put the eyes in."

"No."

Mel sat up and leaned over. "He's the kid in that photo, right? The one that spooked you at Sister Jerome's place."

"The one you've been seeing in your dreams," Jo said. "Right?"

"Right." His mouth tightened.

"So that's got to mean something. I mean, that I saw him too."

Calvin tore the page off and started to crumple it, but Jo grabbed it away from him. She smoothed it out and studied it. "I saw him fall into the pool. But he wasn't pulled in, like the others. He tried to get his toy soldier and he broke through the ice. I wonder…"

"They must have kept records of all the deaths," Calvin said.

"I bet they did. D'you still have Sister Jerome's card?"

CALVIN WAS HALFWAY across the lawn toward the garage to get the card when the land line phone rang in the house. Mel scrambled to answer it, then came back to the door. "It's Aunt Frieda."

Jo sat up. "How's Lew?"

"Better every hour, she says. She wants to talk to you."

"Me?" Jo pushed herself to her feet. Her legs felt like rubber.

The telephone was a scuffed red model from the 1990s that hung on the kitchen wall near the door. Frieda's voice was bright and cheerful. "I can't believe how much he's improving! Jo, I'm so glad you and the others helped me get him to the hospital in time. If you hadn't…" Her voice caught, then she went on. "He's strong enough to speak, a little. He's actually said a few words."

"That's wonderful!" She shot a smile at Mel, who stood at her elbow, and Calvin, a pace back, his face shuttered.

"Yes, but the strange thing is, the first word he said was your name."

"Gosh! I must have made an impression." Jo put a smile in her voice.

"He was half dreaming, I think. It was late last night. He seemed to be worried about you. I told him you were fine, and that calmed him. But since then I've been thinking … better make sure."

Jo stared at the wall next to the phone. Here was her chance to tell Frieda what had been happening. What was still happening. Make her understand why they could never bring Lew back to Spinbrook House.

"Jo? Are you all right?"

No. The truth was too fantastic. Frieda would never believe.

"Of course I'm all right," she said cheerfully. "Tell Lew not to worry. Tell him I'll come and see him soon, if that's allowed."

"Of course it's allowed. But if all goes well, maybe you won't have to come here. The doctors say we may be able to bring Lew home tomorrow!"

"Bring him home tomorrow!" She glanced at Mel, who shook her head. "Wow, that's — that's amazing!"

"We'll have a party! Just a quiet little one, for Lew."

"You bet! That'll be just — just great!"

She put the phone down. "You heard?"

Mel nodded. "Not much time left," Calvin said.

"Right. Sister Jerome."

He held up the card. It was austerely printed, black on white, with ST. INNOCENT HOUSE in the centre and below that, much smaller, SR. JEROME TIMMINS. Phone number and email address in one corner, street address in another. The only graphic, centred near the top, was a small line drawing of a flying dove, like the one on Jeremy's medal.

She punched in the number. Two rings, and the phone at the other end was snatched up and a voice lilted, "St. Innocent! Jerome speaking!"

Jo had been nervous, but now she found herself smiling. "Hi, Sister Jerome. It's me, Jo Meurig. D'you remember — "

"You bet I do! You and Calvin Ransom! You got something new for me?"

"Well, no, actually we were hoping for something from you."

"Oh. You mean about Ellen Quinn? Sorry, I'm just getting into that."

"No, not that. Um..." How to put this? "Remember that group photo you showed us? With the young boy, the little one with dark hair who stood by himself?"

"The one that gave Calvin such a scare?"

Jo swivelled to raise eyebrows at Calvin. "Yes, that one. I think I know what happened to him."

"Really! You've been doing some digging, eh?"

"Not exactly." She looked from Calvin to Mel, saw no help there. "I, um, I can't explain how I found out. But if you have time, could you please see if there's a record of a kid who was drowned in the pool near the orphanage around the time of that photo?"

"Yeah," Sister Jerome said slowly. "I'm writing this down. And I'm wondering..."

"It would have been in early or late winter, when the ice was forming or else breaking up. I think he broke through the ice and that's how he drowned."

"Huh. Wow." Jo could picture Sister Jerome staring, those sharp eyes needling the air.

"Yes, and if you could find out more and let us know, that would be great. Actually," she added, "it could be really important."

A beat of silence, then: "Well, phoo. Mysterious! Do I ever get told what this is all about?"

"Yes," Jo said firmly. "Only right now there's no time."

Another beat of silence, then: "Okay, I'm on it. Soon's I find out anything I'll phone. If there's anything like a photo I'll send it by cell phone. Got one?"

"No. There's a computer here we can use, though. Could you send it by email? I just have to run upstairs and find out the address, and — "

"I know the address," Mel said in Jo's ear.

Jo covered the speaker with her hand. "I thought you weren't allowed to use that email."

Mel shrugged and rolled her eyes. Jo passed on the address to Sister Jerome.

"I bet she wants to know how you knew," Calvin said, after she hung up.

"And I'll tell her. When this is over."

Chapter 27

"WHEN THIS IS OVER!" Mel gave herself a shake and led the way out the front door. "It's like being in a war. Even if we do find out what happened to that boy, what good will it do us?"

"We still don't know enough. We need to know as much as possible. Knowledge is power, right? Besides, I have a feeling he's important." Jo folded down onto her blanket in the sun. "There is one other person we can ask. If he survived."

"Your invisible writer?" Calvin had his sketchbook out again and was working on a fresh sheet. With a few quick strokes, another face took shape. A boy about fifteen, thin, serious eyes, light hair.

"You've got magic fingers!" Jo leaned in. "Who is that?"

Mel knelt up to get a look. "I know that face." She squinted. "No... yes... sorta...."

"Wait a sec," Jo said. "That looks like..." She gazed from Calvin's averted face to the pictured face, all eyes and anxiety. "It's you, right? When you were younger?"

"Nope."

"Yes it is!" Mel slapped his arm.

"No. I thought it was at first, but then I figured it out." Calvin dropped the sketch on the grass and offered Jo a grave smile. "My Great-granddad Jeremy has been talking to me."

He told them about seeing the boy's reflection in glass and mirrors, and about the warnings. "That's how I knew you were in danger at the pool, that second day."

"Gosh." Jo rolled back on her blanket. "So he's been dead and gone... how long?"

"More than forty years."

"But he still seems to think it's his job to watch out for people around here?"

"His ghost!" Mel whispered. "Protecting us! Way cool!"

"The ghost of his younger self, anyway," Calvin said.

Jo picked up the sketch and studied it. "Keeping watch. Trying to keep people safe. But why would he — or his ghost — be stuck at just that age?" She lowered the picture. "Wait a minute—"

"Sounds like your pen pal," Calvin said.

"Yes!" Mel sat up. "And if he was Jeremy, that would mean *it* didn't get him, anyway. We know Jeremy lived a long life."

"Yes, but I haven't had a word from him since that last time," Jo said. "I wish I could get to him! He might have learned something that would help us."

Mel jumped up and went into the house. Two minutes later she was back, with Jo's journal and pen in her hand.

Jo settled herself cross-legged, opened her journal on her knee, and began an account of what happened last night, so far as she could remember. There were a lot of gaps. *I feel like a fool now,* she wrote. *Because Lew knew what to do, and he was braver than me. He tried to help me, when I should have been trying to rescue him. And he was smart enough to see that the other boy was dangerous.* A chill swept over her as she recalled being pulled into the dark pool. *Strength in numbers,* she wrote. *It seems to be true. The minute Lew and I got together, we were stronger. I felt we could have broken free, both of us, if we'd got our act together in time. Here, we're three. That makes us even stronger. And three is a lucky number.*

She paused, pen in air. All three watched the blank page. Nothing happened. Jo tossed the pen onto the grass and clapped the book shut.

"Write some more," Calvin said.

"No, he's nowhere near. I feel it. There's nothing." She tried to see what he was drawing now. He turned his sketchbook away from her, but not before she caught a glimpse of a face that looked like hers, only just a tad (she thought) prettier. She suppressed a grin of pleasure. "Hey! I've got an idea. Remember what you said the other day about how your paintings are a door to let something out?"

He gave her a guarded look.

"Well, last night, one of them was a door to let something in, wasn't it?"

"Mm." He scowled.

"Do you think maybe you could open another door? For Jeremy?" She opened her journal to a blank page and held it out. Calvin leaned back from it as if it might bite him. Then he sighed, shrugged, took the journal, braced it on his knee, and began to sketch.

Mel and Jo leaned in on either side of him. Jeremy's face took shape with a few strokes. "That does look like you," Jo murmured. The face was looking away from them a little, and tilted downward, as if he was intent on something below him. Then Jo realized: He's writing in his journal. This is the other half of what I saw.

Calvin inhaled and jerked his hand away from the page. The last stroke of charcoal swooped away from Jeremy's sketched face and began to form words in a familiar spiky script. .... *fire against ice. But I'm scared even that will not work for long. We cant kill it. Marie says we need to find its lair.* ["Marie!" Calvin laughed. Jo: "What?" Calvin: "My great-grandmother's name." Jo: "Ah-hah!"] *If we could find it, then perhaps then we could do something — although what, I don't know. I am dead sure now that the heart of its power lies deep, but near. Nearer even than the pool. The sisters keep the cellar locked up, and sometimes I have wondered if they are afraid of that*

---

great boulder in the foundation. I have seen it twice, and it scares me to pieces. The danger place is there — only not there, but und—

Jo yelled and fell backward as the journal exploded off Calvin's knee. Mel shrieked. The book fell to the grass in a flutter of torn pages. They gathered around it at a safe distance and watched, but it didn't move again. Calvin bent and picked it up gingerly, by the edges of the cover, and opened it to his sketch of Jeremy. That page, and the two or three behind it, hung in ribbons. The slashes made Jo think of pointed fingernails.

"Somebody didn't like what Jeremy was telling us," she said. "That means it's something we should know."

"The danger place," Mel said shakily. "The great stone in the foundation — he must mean the hearthstone. He — he must mean the cellar, where...." She sat down on the grass and wrapped her arms around her knees.

"No, he started to write *under*. I think he means deeper than the cellar," Jo said. "That must be — "

Calvin waved the ripped journal in the air. "You're both missing something important. Look around you!" He swept out an arm. The two girls gave him blank looks, and then Jo said, "Oh..."

"It's broad daylight!" He let the book thump to the ground. "The thing attacked us right out in the sunshine! Think how much stronger it's got since yesterday."

"Since it almost got Jo," Mel muttered, not looking at her.

Jo felt cold all over. "You think it's my fault?"

Calvin sat down beside her and slipped an arm around her shoulders. "Of course not. But what it means is..." His arm tightened. "It's strongest by night, right? How much stronger will it be tonight?"

"So..." Jo cleared her throat. "If we're going to do anything, we'll have to do it now." But she wasn't near ready. She was weak and scared and tired, and...

"If we don't...." Calvin rubbed his hair into a tangle. "By tomorrow, when Lew gets home, maybe the best we'll be able to do is run away."

"That's if we survive tonight. Look, I don't know about you two, but I can't run away, even if I wanted to. Cal — "

"I'm with you."

"Me too, I guess," Mel said gloomily. She picked up her blanket and shook it out. "So what's the plan?"

"There's no time for anything fancy," Jo said. "If we want to save Lew's life, and — and maybe our own, we need to find its lair, like Jeremy said. And we have to do it today." She glanced at the sun, already halfway down the sky. "Before it gets dark."

Mel swung the blanket around her shoulders and pulled it close. "Find its lair! How?"

"It's obvious now, don't you think?" Jo looked at Calvin.

"Under the hearthstone, like Jeremy says," he said. "We already knew there's something under there, some space, by the way the groundwater flows down."

"And you, Mel, you told me this whole area's honeycombed with caves. And there's that extra cold current in the dark pool."

"You think maybe there's a connection between the pool and the hearthstone?" Mel shivered. "But how are we going to find it? You can't see anything in that pool! And besides, who would be crazy enough to go back in there with that... *whatever*... lurking?"

Jo's heart thudded. Her ankle throbbed with cold. "The three of us," she said firmly. "It would be crazy for one, but we three could do it together. Strength in numbers."

"Light would help a lot," Calvin said. "Not a regular flashlight. We'd need a diver's lamp, a good bright one."

"You've got such a thing?"

"No, but I know where I can get one. There's a store in Burfast that rents diving gear. I can be there and back in less than an hour."

JO STOOD WATCHING until the Ford station wagon was out of sight. Mel squinted up at the sky. "Sunset's around eight-thirty."

"Lots of time," Jo said, more confidently than she felt. "Can't be much more than six."

"You're not really serious about this?"

"Can you think of another plan?"

"But, I mean, what about your..." Mel lowered her voice, as if someone might overhear. "You know. Your fear of dark water."

Jo forced a smile. "I'm trying hard to think about Lew. Not about the pool. Or — or things that happened before. Don't make it harder!"

"I'm sorry, but I ..." Mel waved her hands in the air. "I'm not brave. This is too much for me."

"Well, we can't do anything till Calvin gets back. Let's stay in the sun as long as we can."

Mel changed into shorts and a shirt, then they walked to MacPhee. They went the long way, by the highway. It took even longer than usual because Jo still hadn't recovered all her energy. But she felt it building up again as she moved and stretched.

She wanted something hot to eat, so they bought pizza slices from the same store that sold ice cream, and sat on the wooden bench outside the store to eat them.

Jo tried not to track the changing angle of the shafts of sunlight that rayed through the trees and between the houses, but she couldn't stop herself. Every minute the shafts slid closer to level and the shadows grew longer. *It's strongest by night.*

It was past seven-thirty as they started slowly back along the highway. Jo kept expecting to hear the growl of the Ford's engine behind them. But by the time they turned in at the gravel drive leading to Spinbrook House, Calvin was still not back.

Chapter 28

AT SEVEN-THIRTY Calvin was standing in a deserted strip mall on the outskirts of Toronto, trying to see in through the darkened windows of the Diving Emporium. It had taken him an hour to drive here from his last stop. "It's a big store, plenty of stock," according to the man who ran Diver's Haven in Burfast, and that appeared to be true. But the store was closed.

Calvin stepped away from the glass and stuck his hands in his jeans pockets, the better to think. He'd driven here because the Burfast store had nothing he wanted to rent and nothing he could afford to buy. "I'm sorry, fella," the man said. "I could sell you a tank and some other gear but my rental equipment's all been taken."

They would need diving lamps, at least one — two would be better — and scuba gear. Wet suits would be good, too, in that icy water. But the shopping list was useless when they couldn't afford to pay for it.

I'll keep looking, he thought, as he walked back to the station wagon. I'll find a phone book. Somewhere in Toronto, there must be a diving store that stays open late and has what we need.

Of course, that would mean he wouldn't be back at Spinbrook House until after sunset. Maybe full dark. That wouldn't be so bad, though. Jo would just have to put off her plan of attack one more day.

He slid behind the wheel and started the engine, and then paused with his hand on the ignition. *But suppose it doesn't wait? Suppose it likes two-to-one odds better than three-to-one?*

Calvin turned out of the parking lot and headed for the highway.

The sun, a red smudge behind city smog, hung a hand's width above the horizon. With each dusty mile it sank lower.

THE SHADOW-STRIPED lawn in front of the house was empty and quiet. The phone rang as they came into the house and Jo, first in the door, snatched it up on the third ring. Sister Jerome's voice lilted in her ear. "Hi there! Jo? Did you get my email?"

"Oh, no. I forgot to check." She mouthed at Mel, *Sister Jerome*. Into the phone: "Did you find out something?"

"Did I! That boy in the photo? His name was Raphael Quinn."

"Quinn." Jo felt a chill. She thought of a gravestone outside a cemetery fence. Mel stared at her.

"Right. Son of Ellen Quinn. Remember that gravestone you found? She was one of the kitchen workers at the orphanage. Got in trouble at the age of 15, poor kid, and had a baby out of wedlock. Named him after an archangel, though the sisters tried to talk her out of that. Still, they were kind to her, in their way. Kept her on staff and raised the boy with the other children. It's all there in the Reverend Mother's personal journal, and the health and school records." Sister Jerome's voice bounced with excitement.

"So what happened?"

"Well…" Her voice lost its brightness. "Raphael vanished. March 3, 1897. He was only six years old. They found a toy of his in the pool, so they thought he probably fell through the ice and was drowned. Just as you said. How did you know?"

"I… um…" Jo floundered.

"Okay, never mind that for now. They never found him. And Ellen was all wrapped up in the kid — he was all she had, I guess. So she went quietly mad and drowned herself two weeks later. The sisters buried her outside the cemetery and put her name on a stone."

After a silence she added, "And that's the end — of a very sad story."

"Sad, yes," Jo murmured. *But not the end.*

"Jo? Is there anything else you want to tell me?"

"N- not now. Not yet. But..." She really didn't want to ask this. "What did Ellen look like?"

"You can see for yourself." The lilt was back in Sister Jerome's voice. "I found a group photo from that era with everybody in it — all the children, the sisters, the help, everybody. I scanned it at a really high resolution and emailed it to you."

Five minutes later Jo was upstairs staring at the computer screen, with Mel leaning over her shoulder. *Kitchen staff are on the left,* Sister Jerome had emailed. *They aren't named, but only one of the four is obviously young enough to be Ellen.*

"Oh..." Jo said. Mel made a sound as if she'd been poked in the stomach.

There she was, right at the end of the row, a little apart from the others. Ellen Quinn. Slender, tall, with masses of cloud-like fair hair twisted up on her head. Jo wondered if that space between her and the others was of her choosing, or theirs. She stood very straight and gazed defiantly at the camera. Her mouth was sad. Her eyes were large and pale, like lights in her face.

"Look." Mel pointed. "Look what she's wearing."

All the kitchen workers wore spotless white dresses and aprons, almost like the sisters' habits, except they had no head coverings. And right in front of Ellen stood the boy, Raphael. Her hands rested firmly on his shoulders. Something about the loving, possessive gesture made Jo shiver.

"Okay." Mel's voice wobbled. "So now we know she wasn't a... a Peg Powler, or... or some kind of monster."

"She wasn't then. She is now."

Jo closed the file and started a new message. She sent thanks, and a question: "When did the high death rate at the orphanage begin?"

"I think we know when," Mel said.

"Sister Jerome has the records. This is for her, not for us — to help her put two and two together. We owe her that."

Mel shuddered violently. "Why am I so cold?"

"Weird, isn't it?" Jo forced a smile into her voice. "We must be kind of in shock. Hey — you know what would be neat? A fire in the fireplace."

"If there's any wood, it would be piled beside the garage."

They found the woodpile. Beside it was a kaleidoscopic heap of broken and splintered paintings. Eyes, hands, faces hacked in two.

"Looks like Calvin's entire output." Jo poked at the fragments with her foot. "So that's what the chopping noise was this morning. He was making damn sure none of them could be used as a door."

"Maybe we should burn them," Mel said. "Finish what he started."

"Fire against ice, heat against cold. Let's do it!"

Armful by armful, they carried the heap into the living room and dumped it on the floor beside the fireplace. Jo was careful to stay clear of the hearthstone and she made sure Mel didn't touch it either. Mel reached across it to build the fire with newspaper and kindling, and side by side they fed the pieces of paintings to the flames.

Details flared to life: a curl of white water, a beckoning hand, a tree branch that seemed to claw at them as the board beneath it crumpled. Faces peered slyly out at them through veils of flame — flames that were green and blue and purple.

"Hm," Jo said, "this isn't as cheery as I thought it would be."

"But the oils make such pretty colours as they burn," Mel said dreamily. She sat with her arms wrapped around her drawn-up knees and gazed into the fire. Her face was flushed, her eyes bright. Jo saw suddenly how dark the room was behind them and how their shadows crawled and leaped with the dancing flames. It must be nearly sunset.

"Where's Calvin got to?" she wondered aloud.

ONLY HALF OF the sun showed above the horizon now. A few miles short of the turnoff to MacPhee, the Ford crawled along behind a tractor-trailer. The left lane was closed for construction, had been for miles, and now it looked like there'd been some accident ahead, forcing the remaining two lanes of traffic into one.

Calvin pounded the steering wheel with his fist. If things had been normal, he'd cover the distance in no time. He'd be at Spinbrook House now. As it was, no way he could get there before dark.

"I HOPE nothing's happened to him," Jo said. She threw another fragment of painting — oil on plywood, this one — on the fire and jumped back as the flames snapped and sparks sprayed. Another face gazed out at her through fire. This was the one that had sent Mel running from Calvin's room the other day. The one with Mel — but not Mel — all in white, on the cellar stairs.

Mel let out a soft sigh. Jo glanced at her and saw her staring at the fragment wide-eyed, as if it was talking to her. "Don't let it freak you out," Jo said. She gave Mel's hand a squeeze. The hand was limp and cold. Mel closed her eyes and turned her face away.

As the flames licked at it, Mel's face in the painting faded into others, a stream of them, one after the other, as if the fire was scrubbing away layers of people. So many faces, some she knew, others who were strangers. Most were children. They rose to life and faded, rose and faded. So many young lives swallowed up. And then there were no more.

"Mel? It's okay. It's all burned now. Nothing left to see."

Mel didn't answer. When Jo turned, she was alone in the room. Uneasy, she went outside. The sun was a red flare in a bright rose sky, low down in the trees to the west. Even as she looked the flare shrank to a sliver, shot up one last crimson beam, and died.

"Mel! Are you out here?" No answer. This didn't feel right. They'd agreed to stay together. Then Calvin had gone off, and now Mel was gone, and they were all split up, each of them alone.

"Mel! Where are you?" Maybe she's still in the house, Jo thought. But before she could step back inside, Mel called from the far side of the house, where the path ran down to the dark pool. Jo ran around the house to the top of the path. Something white — looked like Mel's T-shirt — flickered below. "Mel!" Jo yelled again, and ran down the path. Halfway down she tripped and would have sprawled headlong, if she hadn't caught at a maple sapling in mid-fall.

A sound came from below. A splash, almost drowned out by the voice of the stream. Jo skidded and stumbled down the path. When she came out from under the trees at the bottom nobody was there. The pool lay in front of her, dull black under the bright sky. One big circular ripple spread out from the centre and lapped at the rocks.

Jo teetered on the edge of the rocks. *She's gone in. Mel — Evan — I have to go in. But I can't — I can't —* Her right ankle and left wrist were cold and stinging where hands had gripped them. The cold spread through her body.

As she balanced there, yellow lights swept through the trees at the top of the hill. The Ford's headlights. Jo shook with relief. She took a step toward the path, then stopped and turned back. She'd already dithered too long, and by the time she got up there and dragged Calvin down here and he'd put on his scuba gear.... *No time! Mel has no time!*

Wait any longer and it would be just like Evan on the South Shore. Dead hands drifting...

One more frozen moment, then she kicked off her sandals and plunged.

Chapter 29

DOWN AND DOWN she speared, and thought at first she had over-shot her target in the dark. Then her groping hand touched cold flesh. A thin shoulder, a cloud of hair like seaweed. *Mel — no — oh God —* She grabbed at the shoulder. A face turned toward her, a face so pale it glowed faintly silver in the dark green gloom. Mel's face, mouth open as if trying to speak, eyes wide with terror. Then she wrenched free of Jo's hands and shot away like an otter.

Jo followed, desperate, her lungs beginning to ache. *What's wrong with her? What did she see when she looked at me?*

Mel was almost out of sight now. Jo caught the flicker of white feet vanishing into a pit of darkness. Chest bursting, close to panic, she surged upward and broke the surface. White foam spread around her across the inky water. She trod water and inhaled huge gulps of air. Then filled her lungs and yelled for Calvin.

He didn't answer, didn't come. He was inside the house, where he couldn't hear her. Looking for her. Going from room to room, turning on lights, transforming the house into a jewelled cage. How long would it take for him to realize neither she nor Mel was there, that something must be wrong? "Calvin!"

She tried to make sense of the last thing she'd seen, that flicker of white feet. Where had Mel gone? Then it hit her. Mel had found the way — the connection between the pool and whatever lay beneath the hearthstone. That had to be it. She'd found the hidden way and she'd gone…

But Mel would never do that. Swim into an underwater tunnel

with a mystery at the other end? Never. Only if she was driven or dragged.

And suppose there was no exit at the other end, and Mel was stuck there, drowning? Like Evan.

Jo trod water and stared up at the glowing house. She fought off panic. *I need a moment. One second, two, and I'll be ready.*

No time!

And she knew she would never be ready, not if she waited hours.

She took three deep breaths, then another, upended, and dove. Here was the sloping side of the pool, and here was the black pit where Mel had gone. An icy current flowed from it. Before her nerve could break again, Jo forced herself at it. As she felt her way past the opening, pushing herself along by hauling at the rocky walls more than actually swimming, she promised herself: It's okay. Nothing to it. If I start needing air, I'll turn back.

Two hammering heartbeats, three... four... Her body moved sluggishly against the current. The water was numbing. And black, so black. She had no sight, nothing but touch, and her hands were clumsy with cold.

This is a mistake. The thought was so clear, she could see it printed in glowing letters across the blackness inside her head. *Go back. Go back now!*

It should have been easy. Just turn around and let the current push her along. But when she tried to turn, the rocky walls were suddenly too close. Her hips and shoulders jammed. One knee scraped painfully on jutting stone. Blackness filled her head.

I'm going to die.

CALVIN STOPPED the Ford in front of Spinbrook House and was out from behind the wheel and inside the house in three seconds. By contrast with the afterglow outside, it was already dark in here. He smelled burned wood. Embers glowed in the fireplace. But nobody was here.

"Jo? Mel?" No answer. The house seemed to echo, the way it does when nobody's home. *Well, they could've gone for a walk, but...*

No. They should be here.

He turned on the lights in the living room, then ran upstairs to the third floor. "Jo!"

All the bedroom doors were closed. He thumped on the first one he came to, then tried the knob. It was locked. Something stirred inside. He thumped again. "Open up! It's me!"

The lock clicked and the door opened a crack, then swung wide. Mel stood there frowning at him. "What took you so long?"

"Traffic. Jo in there?"

"No, Jo's downstairs burning stuff in the fireplace. You know, paintings. Bits." She wiggled her fingers. "I kind of freaked. Some of the bits were...."

"Jo's not downstairs."

"Then she's in her room. Calvin, guess what? We found out who that boy was. He... Calvin, wait!"

Something was wrong, he felt it like an itch under his skin. He dashed along the corridor and flung open Jo's door, switched on the light. Nobody there. Same with Lew's room. He crossed to poke his head out on the terrace. Empty. He ran back along the corridor and checked the bathroom. Empty.

Down to the second floor gallery, check all the rooms. Empty, empty, empty.

Back on the first floor he detoured to the kitchen, to be thorough, then crossed the living room and looked down into the Cataract

Room. It was getting dark. The embers in the fireplace had gone out.

As he stood in front of the fireplace, thinking, it occurred to him to wonder why it was so cold here. The coals should still be radiating heat. Instead, he'd almost swear they were radiating cold. He bent and held a hand above the burned-out fragments. Then knelt and touched them.

His fingers came up crusted with soot and frost. Icy cold bit through the knees of his jeans. He scrambled backward, away from the hearthstone.

"What is it?" Mel stood at the foot of the stairs, watching him and shivering. "What's happening?"

"I don't know. I wish I could find Jo."

"There's only two other places she could be, and she wouldn't go to either of them, not now." Mel looked at the darkening windows. "The cellar, and — "

"The pool. No, she wouldn't go there." But the moment the thought was out he knew, and he was out the door. The pool: the place he should have looked first.

Coming out at the bottom of the path, he saw... "Oh, no. No." A pair of sandals lay close to the edge, one of them upside-down, as if she'd kicked them off. Even in this dim light he could see a fan of water droplets flung across the stones.

He kicked off his shoes and shed his heavy jeans and was deep in the pool a moment later. But as he groped through the thickening gloom, he knew there was next to no chance of finding Jo this way. And even if he did find her, it would be too late.

INSTINCT SCATTERED common sense. Instead of trying to push backward toward the tunnel opening, Jo pushed upward, toward what would have been the surface if she'd been outside, with precious air above it, and…

And found it. Air, moist and stinking of algae, but sweeter than any perfume she'd ever smelled. Exploring with her hands, she found the rough walls of the tunnel still close around her body. They slanted in above her head. She felt up and couldn't feel where they met. Not a tunnel, then. More like a crevasse.

Air, wonderful air. Jo spent a minute just breathing and feeling thankful. She hoped Mel had discovered this breathing space.

The thought of Mel started Jo moving again. But everything was different now. With the terror of drowning at least temporarily under control she felt equal to anything. Even to feeling her way like this, half-swimming, half-clambering on slippery rocks, through a bruising, water-loud darkness.

The darkness was the worst part now. She saw nothing except for the splotches and squiggles of light drifting inside her eyes. Sometimes the splotches looked like faces: oval, phosphorescent greenish white, with dark pits for eyes.

Then came the place where the rocky roof came down close over her head and slanted into the water in front. Her breathing space had come to an end. The real tunnel lay in front.

She croaked aloud, to give herself courage: "I haven't found Mel yet, so she must have gone in there. That means I can go in there too. Besides, the place under the cellar, if there is one, must be close. I must be nearly there."

If there is such a place. If this tunnel doesn't end in a trap.

Panic crept up on her again, flexing its claws. She had to move. *Yes, move. Go back!*

But... That thing Evan said, what was it? You have to go through the darkness to reach the light. It's the only way.

Go on, then. Go on.

At that moment Jo noticed something. She could see her hand on a knob of rock. Light! Radiating from under the water, from somewhere ahead in the tunnel. It must have been very dim, but after that intense blackness it struck her eyes like a flood of sunshine.

First air, then light. Yes!

But the light was nothing like sunshine. It was cold, dead, greenish. And horribly familiar. If Mel had reached the place where the tunnel came out, then she wasn't alone.

Go!

She breathed deeply and steadily, saturating her lungs with oxygen. Then drew one more breath, held it, and headed down. The cold light brightened moment by moment. Then it was radiating down from above her, from beyond a silvery surface, and she surged upward and broke out into the air once more. Space opened around her. Her feet found stony ground and she waded ashore.

So, she'd found it. What had Jeremy called this place? Lair, stronghold, the centre of its power. The danger place. Yet he had also called it "its heart." She wondered what he'd meant by that.

God help me. It's like the North Pole in here. Her breath smoked, her ice-stiffened clothes chafed her numb body. She was standing on the shore of a small island a couple of metres across, at the centre of a low-roofed cavern. A massive boulder — it had to be the hearthstone — grounded itself in front of her. She wondered if this was its real base, or did the pillar continue downward?

A stream spilled from a crack in the wall beyond the hearthstone, divided to go around the island, and flowed out through a gap in the opposite wall: the way she'd come in. The stream and the rocks at its edges, and the boulder, too, glowed with that same deadly moonwhite light she'd seen in Lew's room by night, the same light she'd glimpsed in the cellar. And the cellar — she looked up — had to be

---

right above her head, with who knew how many tons of rock between there and here.

Jo had time to notice these details, because her first glance had shown her Mel was not here.

But I saw her go into the tunnel ahead of me! There was no way either of them could have missed the other in that narrow space. *Okay, I get it. I didn't see Mel. I saw... something else.* But the something else was not here, either.

She wondered where the light was coming from. And why was it so cold in here? Both answers came together when she looked closely at the glistening rocks edging the stream. Ice. And the hearthstone was coated in it. The light came from the ice.

There was something in the ice, at the base of the hearthstone, where a dip in the island made a hollow for ice to pool. Something about the size of... Jo knelt and tried to see through the whitish murk.

About the size of a child. Here was the mop of fine dark curls. Here was the thin dark-clad body, curled in a fetal position.

Got to get him out! She hit the ice with her fist. It didn't even show a crack. She only hurt her hand. *Got to get him out. He can't breathe in there!*

It came to her that she wasn't using very many brain cells, because of course he wasn't breathing. Every part of her, including her mind, had turned heavy and slow.

It's the cold. I'm freezing to death.

Brightness shone from somewhere behind her and reflected from the stone. She climbed to her feet, nursing her bruised fist. Turned around. One long stride away, at the edge of the water, stood the shining white figure that had held Lew in a gentle embrace, the night he had nearly died. Its smile was heartbreakingly sweet and loving.

Come, said a silvery voice in Jo's mind. *Come to me. You belong with me.*

No!

Yes. It stretched out sharp-tipped hands. Jo had not the strength to resist as the long, white arms gathered her close, as a nurse or a mother gathers a sick child, and cradled her gently. The sweet and terrible face bent above her. *Hush... hush....*

Chapter 30

WHEN CALVIN finally swam to shore and crawled out, exhausted, onto the rocks, Mel was sitting on a rock waiting for him. She wiped tears off her face with both hands. "You're not going to find her, are you?"

He yanked on his jeans. "Get to a phone! The nearest OPP detachment is in Burfast. They'll send divers."

Mel was on her feet instantly and racing up the path. Calvin put on his shoes and trudged up the path after her, Jo's sandals hooked on one hand. Speed couldn't help her now. Nothing could help her.

He looked into the glass walls as he rounded the front of the house. With the lights on, the windows made no mirrors. No chance for that half-grown blond kid to offer useful hints. Not that his hints had been much help so far. *Jo's gone. And I couldn't stop it from happening.*

Seeing the staircase reminded him that there was one place he hadn't checked. The cellar. Not that he expected to find her there, but at least when the police arrived he could say he'd searched everywhere. Trudging mechanically, one foot after the other, stone-heavy with despair, he went to the garage to get the big flashlight, then into the house and down the cellar stairs.

Halfway down he stopped. Cold white light filled the stairwell. It leaked from the cracks around the cellar door. A warning flared in his brain. *Get away now!*

But if Jo was in there…

He took a firm grip on the flashlight, holding it like a weapon —

as if that was any use — stepped cautiously down the stairs, and opened the door.

The cellar was deserted. He made sure of that, first thing. But it was different. The low, dark space was not dark: it was a blur of white light. And colder than January. Floor, walls, ceiling, sparkled with frost. The hearthstone shone under a coat of ice. The rivulets trickled under shining jackets.

Calvin's wet shirt stiffened on him as it froze. He walked two or three stunned steps out into the middle of the space, gaping around. And then understanding smacked him in the head.

Jo. It had taken Jo — all her stubborn courage and fierce protectiveness, all her life and strength. So much life, burning-bright, and now it had stolen all that. That was how it had become so much stronger.

In despair and fury Calvin hurled the flashlight at the hearthstone. It bounced off in a shower of glass and ice fragments and rolled across the slick floor. He sat down and buried his head on his crossed arms.

"That was a big help, eh?" said a young voice close to his ear.

"Go away. We can't do anything now."

"Why not?"

Calvin looked up and around. The flaxen-haired boy, or his image, frowned out from the shiny ice that sheathed the hearthstone. "Well?"

"We've lost. It got Jo."

"Not yet."

"What?" Calvin scrambled to his feet.

"The thing's got her, but she's not gone. She's fighting. Not like you."

"Where is she? What can I do?" He kicked the flashlight so it ricocheted off the hearthstone, knocking off more ice fragments.

"You could try using your gift," Jeremy said sternly. "'Stead of smashing things."

"Gift?"

"Pictures."

"Oh, that."

"A door to let things in or out, remember? Like she said."

"Right!" Calvin spun and sprinted for the doorway.

"Wait! Where you goin'?"

Calvin pulled up short. "All my supplies are upstairs." He patted his shirt and found the sodden box of charcoal. "Except this."

"No time! You gotta do it now!"

"But — " Okay. He had the charcoal. Now he needed a surface. Floor, walls — too rough. Hearthstone — covered with ice.

"Ice breaks."

"Go away. I know what I'm doing." Calvin used the flashlight to scrape clean a space on the surface of the hearthstone. Jeremy mouthed *Hurry!* at him, then vanished with the scrapings. Calvin got to work.

No need to stop and think what to draw. Jo, of course. He knew that face by heart. The firm chin, tilted up a little, always a challenge there. A sparkle in the eyes — a joke she was willing to share, if you gave her an opening. Curve of jaw, curl of ear, crop of dark red hair, only here it was not red, but black and stone-colour…

No, it wasn't.

Calvin sat back. The picture was coming alive. Colour seeped into it, and warmth. More ice melted around it. Then she moved, turned her head, and caught his eye. Her mouth opened.

Calvin!

"I'm here in the cellar! Where are you?"

I'm… Her eyes moved, looked beyond him. *Calvin, watch out!*

He didn't have time to turn. He only had time to see a brighter light reflected off the stone in front of him, blotting out Jo's face and blinding him. And then a wave of cold on his back, and a hand on his shoulder.

MEL CURLED UP in the leather chair and listened to the noises from below. Calvin was down there, breaking things. She had gone to the top of the cellar stairs, thinking to help, but she'd seen the dead white light and felt the cold radiating upward, and backed away.

I can't go down there. I can't.

Things were quiet now. Even the voice of the falls sounded muffled. Far, far away in the night, something howled. Wolves, or alarm sirens. Could be either.

Every light in the house was on. Strange, then, that the room was growing so dark.

I have to get away from here. But she was so cold, so stiff. She struggled to get on her feet, then sank back and curled up again.

When the hand touched her arm, she was too numb to be afraid. It almost came as a relief when the cold surrounded her, gathered her up in gentle arms, and carried her away.

Chapter 31

JO DROPPED from a blizzard of white light into a frigid darkness. Afraid to open her eyes, she kept them tight shut and took stock. *On my feet, barely. Hands and feet numb. I'm holding onto a... feels like a tree trunk. Squashed against it. Something's dragging at me.*

She opened her eyes. A wintry landscape surrounded her. She clung to a birch tree at the bottom of a hill beside an inky black pool. Ice crusted the rocks beside the pool and glazed its surface. The light on the hillside was dim and cold as starlit snow.

She'd been here before. "At least I'm out of that cave," she said aloud.

"You're not," said a child's voice at the level of her elbow.

Looking down to see who was sharing her tree, Jo wasn't surprised to find Lew. "Your body is still in the cave," he explained gravely and clearly, as if to a person with a slightly muddled brain. "Mine is in the hospital. Calvin's and Mel's bodies are in the house." He nodded up the hill, to where two figures came sliding down, hand in hand. "Just the spirit parts of us are here."

Jo reached out as Calvin and Mel slid level with her. "Over here!" A moment later they were all four clinging to each other and encircling the tree. Calvin reached around Lew to slip an arm around Jo's shoulder. She leaned into him and they snugged Lew between them. Mel got a grip on an arm of each, closing the circle. Ghostly shapes drifted past them and slid into the pool.

"What is this place?" Mel demanded.

"It's the in-between place," Lew said.

Calvin said: "In between what?"

"Life and death," Lew said matter-of-factly. "I've been here lots."

"You mean," Mel quavered, "we — we're dying?"

"Yes. But we're not dead yet. Not like them." Lew pointed at the ghosts sliding into the pool feet first and sinking down like statues, stiff and unresisting.

"So we still have a chance." Jo smiled into Calvin's face, so close to her own. He smiled back. The fact that they could both smile, in this place, gave her heart.

"A chance for what?" Mel said.

"To get away," Jo answered. She looked down at Lew. "Remember the last time we were here? You and I together, we were nearly strong enough to break free."

"Now there's four of us," he said.

"So together we should be strong enough to get away from her."

"Her?" Calvin echoed. "You mean *it*."

"No, her. Ellen Quinn."

"You're kidding!"

Jo almost laughed. "There's no hag. It's a woman. It was a woman, once, I mean." She told him what Sister Jerome had discovered.

"So she was human once." Calvin looked around at the winter landscape and the dark pool. "But this is what she is now. She's changed into something that sucks up people's lives."

"Like a vampire," Mel breathed. "And you guys, think! She's getting stronger all the time!"

"Then let's go now." Jo's hand tightened on Calvin's arm. "Okay? Join up! Calvin, you grab Lew's left hand. Mel, you take his right, and keep hold of my other hand. Come on!"

They formed a ragged line, Calvin on one end, then Lew, Mel, and Jo. Bending against the pond-ward pull, they struggled uphill. Jo thought the first few steps might burst her heart, if that were possible here. Then step by step, the drag eased. "We're going to make it!" Calvin shouted. Lew cheered.

"Suppose — " Mel gasped, "something's — coming — after us?"

Jo grabbed a look back. "There's nothing," she began. Then spotted a boy standing on the edge of the pool. She stopped climbing. Mel staggered backward.

It was the boy in the dark old-fashioned clothes, the boy from the old photograph. The one who had nearly dragged her in to drown, last time. Only, this time he had a name.

"Jo, get moving!" Calvin shouted.

"It's Raphael! We can save him too! We can do it together!"

"He's not alive! You can't save him."

"Well, somebody should have saved him the first time. Then none of this would have happened."

"It's done now." Mel pulled at her arm. "We can't change the past."

"But…" She looked downhill again. The boy was taking his first step out on the ice. It was happening all over again. "We can't just let him drown!"

The ice cracked. The boy went in up to his waist. He screamed in terror.

Jo dropped Mel's hand. Sliding down the hill much faster than she'd climbed it, she fetched up at the bottom and fell to her knees. She got an arm lock on one of the rocks at the edge — the same one she'd held onto last time, maybe — and reached out to the floundering boy. "Grab on!"

He snatched at her wrists and quick as that, he changed. His eyes... *Don't look at his eyes!*

"Jo, let go of him!" Calvin was suddenly beside her, prying at the boy's grip. Mel was trying to free her other hand.

"No! Grab him, not me! Help me pull him out!"

"Jo — "

"Now!" she shrieked.

For a moment everything hung still. Then Calvin started pulling at one of the boy's arms, and Mel pulled the other, and Lew locked his hands around an elbow and strained backward.

Out he came, inch by inch, heavy as a full-grown man. And as he came he changed again, became a terrified small boy. When they had him free of the water Calvin picked him up in his arms. Jo and Mel each took Lew by a hand.

"This time for real," Calvin said. "Go!"

Three paces away from the dark pool, its drag dwindled to nothing. Jo thought even the light was brighter. "We're doing it," she whispered. "We're going to win!"

"Think so?" Mel said faintly. "Look up there."

Jo looked up. Her hand tightened on Lew's. A tall shape stood at the top of the hill looking down at them. It glowed with a dead white light, that darkened the woods all around. It moved down the hill toward them and with each step it grew taller, its face more terrible.

Lew hid his face against Jo's shirt. Calvin stepped back next to her. Mel crowded in on her other side. The child stirred in Calvin's arms and cried out weakly. At the sound the hunger in the woman-thing's empty eyes grew ferocious.

They were almost within the reach of those bone-thin arms. The stink of stagnant water came with it. Jo groped for something they could use against the thing, some weapon, and found none.

Instead she found a gift.

"You — you aren't a thing. You were a woman. Y-your name was Ellen Quinn. Your little boy was Raphael. I — I know what you want."

Dead silence. Even the stream's voice was muted. Then the woman-thing said, its voice whispery and liquid, "I want my boy alive again."

"Y- yes, but he's dead — you can't change that. You're both dead." Jo held her breath. The terrible face, all sweetness and famine, gazed down at her. Then the empty eyes moved to the child in Calvin's arms.

"I, um, think..." Calvin said.

Jo held out her hands, pleading and warding. "Yes, here's — here's your boy. Here's Raphael. We — we're giving him back to you. Safe and sound."

Calvin held out the child, then bent and placed him on the ground. The boy curled up into a fetal position at their feet. Calvin stepped back quickly and seized Jo's hand. She squeezed it hard. The thing — it was still nothing human — curled itself down like a snake and straightened up with the child in its white arms. Then it turned the dark pits of its eyes on Jo.

"Lost," it whispered. "Still lost."

"No! Not lost. I... I know where he is, now," Jo stumbled on. "I — I'll tell people. We can't change what happened, but we can — we *will* bring you together. I promise!"

The invisible gaze held her like a hand on the back of the neck. "You have promised."

Promisssed.... The word faded like a final breath. The dead-white radiance died. The wintry woods darkened. Jo couldn't see the woman-thing holding the child, couldn't see Calvin, couldn't feel his hand.

"Calvin? Mel? Lew!"

Faint cries like echoes answered, and then there was only the silence and the dark.

Chapter 32

JO SAT UP. Stone was cold and gritty under her hands. The darkness was absolute, but now there was sound: water flowing and tinkling and dripping. She felt a little way around her. Stone, nothing but stone.

"I'm back in the cave." Her voice was loud in her own ears.

Reaching out again, her hands found the hearthstone. No ice on it. And it seemed to her it wasn't as cold in here as it had been before. "So maybe I won't freeze to death after all. That's a plus."

She was alone. She was sure of it. Nothing, visible or invisible, was anywhere near her.

She moved her hands down the hearthstone, then remembered what she'd seen lying at its base. Had that been illusion, or real? She didn't want to find out. Careful not to touch anything there, she shifted away. Her left foot splashed into water. It was still as icy as meltwater in March.

"I can get out of here," she told herself, loudly and firmly. "I can! All I need is a little light." It must still be night out there. She wondered if morning would make a difference. If she would even know when it was morning.

Through darkness to the light, the only way.

"Oh, Evan. I wish you were here with me!"

But there must be someone near. Someone who wonders where I am. Calvin?

A dead-still moment, then: *Jo?*

It was only a ghost of a whisper in her head, but she was sure...

almost sure....

She stood up unsteadily, filled her lungs and screamed: "Calvin!"

A long pause, then: "Jo! Where are you?" The voice came mosquito-faint from what seemed miles above. She remembered the crack in the cellar floor.

"I'm below you, I think!" she shouted. "Right by the hearthstone. There's a cave down here!"

"Are you all right?" came the distant voice.

Jo hugged herself in the dark. She was starting to shake. "Yeah, but... I really, really want out!"

Another pause, then: "The police are here. Hold tight!"

"Wait! Tell them there's a tunnel in the north side of the pool. But it's probably too tight for their tanks and stuff. Tell them all I need is a really bright light at the mouth of the tunnel!"

"You sure?"

"Yes! Just a bright light! And Cal— " Her voice broke. "Calvin, please hurry!"

"I THINK — THIS — is what we call — a delayed reaction," she said fifteen minutes later, between hiccupping sobs. Calvin cradled her blanket-wrapped body against his shoulder and rocked her back and forth.

"We've won!" Mel did a little dance beside the pool. "It's all over!"

"Not exactly." Jo watched the police diver unstrapping his scuba gear. "They'll still have to go in and get Raphael. Whatever's left of him is in there. I don't know how he got in the cave, but that's why he was never found." Jo sagged against Calvin, too spent to stay upright.

"We'll have to do something about his bones," Calvin said.

"They have to be together," Jo said, as clearly as she was able. "Him and his mother. I promised."

"And you can bet she'll hold you to it," Calvin said quietly.

IT TOOK LONGER than they wanted — three weeks — to settle things. Not only the legalities, but to have Ellen Quinn's grave and marker moved inside the iron fence of MacPhee Cemetery, and to prove the identity of the child's bones by DNA testing of both sets of remains. "We'll rebury them together," Sister Jerome said happily, "and as soon as possible we'll add Raphael's name and dates to Ellen's stone."

"And will you put their story in that book you're writing about the St. Innocents?" Jo asked.

"I sure will. Or as much of it as I can back up with evidence. The rest of what you told me may have to remain a Mystery."

Jo smiled, hearing the capital M.

The ceremony took place on a drowsy-warm day in the last week of August. As Jo, Mel and Calvin waved goodbye to Sister Jerome and the two other sisters who had come with her and walked away from the cemetery, rich colour caught Jo's eye. "Look!" She pointed into the woods beside the path. "Goldenrod. Fall will be here before we know it."

"Summer's always too short," Mel said glumly.

"I can't believe you're feeling nostalgic. There were times I thought this would be the shortest summer of my life — and the last!"

Calvin walked with his hands in his pockets and said nothing.

They drove back to Spinbrook House in the Ford station wagon. As they pulled up in front of the house, a small boy in jeans and a striped jersey pushed himself up out of a chair under the pergola and waved his arms. He was shouting something.

Three weeks, Jo thought, and look at him. Still not too steady on his feet, still not too strong, still too thin, but full of life and energy. And his voice had come back, a little more every day.

"Got to show you something!" he shouted as they piled out of the car. "The pool!"

"What about the pool?" Jo felt a chill. "You didn't go down there by yourself, did you?"

"Sure I did. Come on!" He grabbed her hand and tugged her toward the path down to the stream. They went down the hill in a procession, Jo and Lew in the lead, then Mel, with Calvin bringing up the rear. At the bottom of the path they came out from under the trees and stood on the rocks at the edge of the pool.

"See?" Lew swept out an arm, proud and excited as if he had accomplished this wonder all by himself. "It happened just now — just half an hour ago."

Jo laughed softly. "I've been waiting for this. I've been down here every day, hoping…"

"Me too," Calvin said.

Mel laughed. "And me."

The dark pool had gone crystal-clear. You could see all the way to the sun-spangled bottom. Nothing there but rocks and silt, a few green weeds shimmying in the current, and a glint of minnows among the green.

"When I get all better I'll swim here," Lew announced.

Calvin caught Jo's eyes and motioned sideways with his head. They walked away along the shore, downstream, leaving Mel and Lew searching for small, flat stones suitable for skimming.

"Something happened to me too, this morning." Calvin raised his voice above the chatter of the stream. "Don't expect me to explain it.

All I know is, for as long as I can remember I've been like a jigsaw puzzle with one piece missing."

"And now?"

"The missing piece is back. No more hollows."

"I'm glad you're better." She smiled up at him. "And the nightmares?"

"None in the last three weeks." He lifted a hand as if to brush a strand of hair from her left eyebrow, then spun away and moved a pace ahead. "You're better too," he said over his shoulder.

"I've been better a while, I think. Ever since the night I got through that tunnel to the cave. You know, through darkness... What Evan tried to teach me."

"No more fear of dark water?"

"Well, I'll always be careful, and who wouldn't? But it doesn't paralyze me any more. It doesn't get into my dreams. I've been all the way along that road, right to the end. I don't have to walk it any more."

"So, uh, I guess," he tossed over his shoulder, "you'll be heading home soon."

"Actually, I should have gone home a week ago," she said to his back. "I just stayed to make sure I could keep my promise to Ellen."

"Ah. Well." He kept on walking, his attention on the uneven rocks beneath their feet.

I wish he would stop and turn around and look at me. I wish he would talk to me. I wish I had the nerve to...

She drew in a deep, steadying breath. *What Evan said. Something in the same spirit, anyway. Only one way out, and that was through. Dive in. Go for it. Aim for the light.*

"Calvin!"

"Mm?" He didn't stop.

Jo skipped ahead and grabbed his arm. "Calvin!"

He swung around. His eyes were laser-blue.

"I lied to you!" she announced.

The eyes narrowed.

"Yes, I lied. My promise to Ellen — that wasn't the only reason I stayed."

The eyes were smiling now, but he wasn't really helping. He waited.

"I, um, I– Oh, for heaven's sake!" She kissed him, and it was a good kiss, and they made it last.

And that was not the end of the story.

About the author

PATRICIA BOW lives in Kitchener, Ontario. She has written more than twenty books for readers of all ages who love mystery, suspense and fantasy. To find out more about Patricia and her work, visit her web page at www.execulink.com/~thebows/patricia.htm.